SIX BLIND MEN AND AN ALIEN

SIX BLIND MEN AND AN ALIEN

MIKE RESNICK

an imprint of

Rockville, Maryland

This story was originally published in the Summer, 2010 issue of Subterranean Magazine

ISBN: 978-1-61242-170-4

www.PhoenixPick.com
Great Science Fiction & Fantasy
Free Ebook every month

Published by Phoenix Pick
an imprint of Arc Manor
P. O. Box 10339
Rockville, MD 20849-0339
www.ArcManor.com

They tell the story about the four blind men and the elephant. One felt the elephant's trunk and declared he was touching a snake. Another felt his leg and concluded that it was a tree trunk. A third felt his tusk and said it was a spear, and the fourth felt its tail and proclaimed that it was a rope...

2038 A.D.

You know, if Papa Hemingway had been around in 2038, he'd have written "The Slush of Kilimanjaro", because that's what he'd have found.

The mountain was a thing of beauty back in 1900. You could see the snow and ice from 80 miles away. By 2000, ninety percent of it had vanished. No one knows why. Or perhaps, like the blind men, everyone knows why, and everyone is wrong.

The Tanzanian government started panicking in 2015. After all, with the game parks depleted of wildlife due to habitat destruction and poaching, the tourists who visited Kilimanjaro were their major source of hard currency. They even tried making snow the way ski lodges do.

It didn't work, of course. They were trying to replace most of a many-miles-long glacier, not provide a path for a handful of skiers.

So more of the snow and ice vanished each year, and by 2038 there sure wasn't a hell of a lot left. But 2038 was a special year, because it marked exactly one century since Ernest Hemingway had written his classic "The Snows of Kilimanjaro", and my sponsor, *Geography Magazine*, decided to fund one last climb up the mountain: "to walk in Hemingway's steps and experience the awe of Kilimanjaro one last time."

Sounded good, even if Papa *hadn't* climbed up past the tree line to the glacier. At least, everyone at *Geography* thought so.

There were six of us, plus the porters.

Jim Donahue was the still photographer. He'd won a number of awards, and his pictures had appeared in just about every prestigious nature and travel magazine in the world.

Adrian Gorman was our guide. He'd climbed the mountain a couple of dozen times, even wrote two books about it. He was the closest thing we had to a celebrity. He knew it, and he acted like it. No one liked him very much, but we trusted him to get us to the top and back down.

Charles Njobo was a representative of the Tanzanian government. (Every expedition had one, which created an extra job for the impoverished country.) He couldn't believe that we'd gone to all this trouble and expense just to see where a long-dead writer had found the corpse of a leopard. He just knew there was something sinister going on, and he was determined to root it out.

Bonnie Herrington was our video camerawoman, tough as nails, dependable as a Swiss watch. I'll never know how she was able to climb that mountain with her eye glued to the viewfinder when most of us could barely do it with our hands and vision unencumbered, but she managed.

Bonnie's sound man, electrician and jack-of-all-trades was Ray Glover, a huge tank of a man who deferred to her every wish. When I asked him why, he explained that she had made him two fortunes already, and he expected her to make him a third one when the documentary of our climb was ready to air.

And there was me — Anthony Tarica. I hold degrees in mammalian biology and botony, so I figured they'd chosen me because it was cheaper than sending a biologist *and* a botonist.

I should also mention Muro, the head porter, a Chagga who knew a bit of English and a touch of German, and was too proud to sleep and eat with the rest of the porters. He always staked out a place halfway between them and us, which corresponded to his position within the safari — but he was destined to play a major role in our adventure.

Most of the conditions below the former snowline haven't changed much. When you hit seven thousand feet, even the tropics can get damned chilly at night — and yet you're only a third of the way to the top.

Three-quarters of the villages are down below you, but you're still in heavy forest, and you've got to watch your step. Even today there are still a few rhino, buffalo and elephant up there, but they're very hard to spot. The brilliant black-and-white colobus monkeys are much easier to see, poor little bastards — that's probably why there are so few left.

At ten thousand feet you can see your breath once the sun starts setting; in fact, if you're exerting yourself, seeing it is almost easier than catching it. There's still an occasional elephant up there, and once in a while a leopard, but most of the animal life at this altitude burrows into the ground or has wings.

At thirteen thousand feet you'd better do most of your breathing through your nose, because the air gets very thin and very dry.

Just short of seventeen thousand feet you hit Kili, where the Chagga tribe lives. They say it used to be covered with snow, but that was half a century ago. The women cultivate the fields. It's too high up for cattle, so there's not much for the men to do, and they spend most of their time not doing it.

Donahue had serious trouble with the altitude and stood, bent over, gasping for air. One of the porters walked over with an oxygen canister, but when he realized that Bonnie had her camera trained on him he waved the man away. "What do you think, Mr. Gorman?" he said.

"I don't think we'll try it today," answered Gorman. "It'll be dark in another hour, too dark to take any photographs. I suggest that we'll stop soon here and start out first thing in the morning."

Donahue finally caught his breath and nodded his agreement. "How the hell did an overweight boozer like Hemingway get up here?"

"He probably didn't," said Gorman.

"Well, I'd like to think that he did," said Donahue stubbornly.

"Would it make any difference if you knew that he didn't?"

"Not a bit. *Geography* says to walk in his steps, either real or presumed." He smiled. "Could be worse. They could have told me to run with the bulls."

"At least we're doing it on their nickel," chimed in Bonnie.

"Their shilling," Gorman corrected her. "You're in British East now."

I looked at the great Adrian Gorman, a legend in his own time, author of two books on his adventures, and actually felt a wave of compassion for him. *You poor son of a bitch,* I thought; *you don't even know whose country this is anymore. It stopped being British East or British anything-else before you were born, for Christ's sake.*

"So we stop here for the night?" asked Donahue.

"Another few hundred feet up the mountain," said Gorman. "There's half a dozen huts there, built to accommodate climbers. They've got some supplies, and they're a hell of a lot warmer than tents. Six of us, six huts. It works out very neatly."

We made it in another half hour.

"Where will the porters stay?" asked Bonnie, looking around.

"They'll use the tents."

"They're going to be awfully cold," she said.

"They're Chaggas," answered Gorman. "They're used to it."

I turned to Muro. "Is that so?"

"Oh yes," he assured me. "Nothing bothers the Chaggas."

"Except the Zanake and the Makonde and the Maasai," said Gorman with a chuckle. "How do you think they wound up so high on this damned mountain?"

Muro stared at him sullenly but said nothing.

"We don't care why the Chaggas climbed the mountain," interjected Ray Glover. "We're concerned with why leopard came up here."

"Not really," Donahue corrected him. "We're concerned with *where* he got to. Hemingway was in charge of *why*."

"Do your readers really care, I wonder?" said Bonnie as one of the porters made the rounds of our party, pouring hot tea for each of us.

"They'd better," said Ray, rubbing his hands together. "An assignment in the Sahara Desert looks pretty appealing right about now."

"It'll look even better when we hit the snow line," said Gorman.

"When do we get there?"

"Sometime tomorrow morning," answered Gorman. "A century ago we'd have been above it since yesterday."

"All I ever saw were pictures," said Ray, "but even so, it's still hard to imagine old Killy without that gorgeous ice cap."

"It'll be even harder for all the tens of thousands of people who live on the lower slopes of the mountain," said Gorman. "That's a lot of water that won't be flowing down to them."

"I just hope that *we* don't flow down to them," muttered Bonnie. "This is a lot steeper than the films I've seen."

"You saw people climbing the Marangu Route," explained Gorman. "That's the easier way to the top."

"Then why the hell didn't we take it?" demanded Donahue. "This isn't supposed to be a feature about the climb, but about what we find."

"The Marangu Route is still in daily use, and no one's found anything," answered Gorman. "We're the first people to take the Mweka Route in more than five years. If Papa's leopard exists, we'll find it here. The way the mountain's melting, they could hardly have missed him if he's anywhere near the Marangu Route."

"You realize," said Charles Njobo, speaking for the first time in hours, "that even if you find this leopard, you are not permitted to move him."

"You say that twice a day," said Bonnie irritably. "Has anyone disagreed with you?"

"Besides," added Ray, "if he's up here, he's been thawing out for years. Who'd *want* to take him home?"

"I am just making sure you understand," said Njobo, a little defensively.

"They understand," said Gorman. He patted his rifle. "Besides, I'll shoot the first one who tries to make off with it."

"You, too?" said Ray. "No one wants to make off with it. Hell, we'll probably smell it long before we see it."

"*If* it's up here at all," added Donahue.

"And on that optimistic note, I suggest we have dinner and get some sleep," said Gorman. "Tomorrow promises to be a long day."

The chef cooked us some kind of very dry, stringy meat that the porters had carted along — I think someone said it was klipspringer – and after we finished we climbed into our huts.

I took my medication — I was the oldest member of the party by a decade, and I had high blood pressure and sky-rocketing cholesterol — and tried to fall asleep. Certainly my muscles were tired enough to go the whole night without even twitching, but I couldn't control my excitement. Up to this point Donahue and Bonnie had done most of the work, but we were getting to the altitude where my expertise would finally be needed. If there *was* a frozen leopard up here, where was he likely to be? That in turn led to the question: what did he eat? Herbivores, obviously — and that meant there had to be herbivores up here before the glacier had turned to slush. If so, what could they themselves have eaten? What kind of plants grew here, and what kind of plant-eaters could they nourish? The leopard would never be too far from his prey, not when he could be seen so easily against the white blanket of the snow, so knowing the habits of his prey would lead me to where he was most likely to have lived and died.

I began going over every variety of plant I had seen that day, sorting them out in my mind, trying to decide which were new to the slope and which might have been there when the glaciers still loomed large — and suddenly I opened my eyes and it was morning, and the camp was bustling with activity.

"Good morning, Professor," said Gorman, who was supervising the making of breakfast.

"Good morning," I said. "And it's Doctor, not Professor."

Gorman shrugged. "Six of one, half a dozen of the other."

Before I could reply, he had walked over to the kitchen area and was berating one of the assistants for breaking the yolks on a pair of eggs.

"I hope we find some elephants or lions up here," said Bonnie softly, joining me as I watched our guide's latest fit of temper. "Otherwise, it's just a matter of time before he starts using the porters for target practice."

"He's supposed to be the best," remarked Ray Glover as he walked by us.

"Well, next time, let's find out the best *what*," said Bonnie. "A century or two back, he'd be carrying a bullwhip and using it on every porter in the party."

"And then wondering why we flinched every time he walked by," added Ray with a smile.

"I'll tell you one thing," I said, and they all turned to me. "I don't like him any better than you do, but I'll bet every member of the party makes it back safely. He doesn't strike me as someone who loses many clients from panic or carelessness."

"You're probably right," said Ray. He flashed us a sudden smile. "My hunch is that he loses 'em on purpose."

We had a quick breakfast of eggs and sausage, and then Gorman got up, clapped his hands twice, and announced that it was time to get started.

"I have a thought," said Jim Donahue. "Why don't we offer a thousand dollar bonus to whoever spots the leopard first? It won't cost us a thing unless someone delivers."

"Bad idea," said Gorman, and I noticed that Charles Njobo was nodding his head in agreement with him.

"Why?"

"The porters are here for our support," said Gorman. "They carry the tents, the food, the tea, the cameras, just about everything else. You offer a thousand dollars for finding a leopard that probably doesn't exist and they'll be all over the mountain, and when we actually do need them they'll be nowhere to be found."

"Okay, point taken," admitted Donahue. "What if we just ask them to look, then, with no reward?"

A truly amused smile crossed Gorman's face.

"Well," he said, "you can *try*."

Muro approached us then, and announced that the tents had been stashed in the huts, the porters had loaded up all the camera and sound gear and the medical kit, and we were ready to continue our ascent of
Kilimanjaro.

"Anyone need any more time?" asked Gorman. "No? Okay then, let's go."

We began climbing, and even though there was hardly enough snow to make a snowman, it was *cold* up there. The air was thin, and within a few minutes we were all panting and gasping. Well, all except Muro and the porters, who seemed to find our discomfort amusing.

Gorman had enough brains — I would never write it off to compassion — to call a break about every half hour and let us catch our breath. It was on the third break, about 9:30 AM, that Muro stared off in the distance, then pulled out his binoculars and held them up to his eyes.

"What do you suppose he sees?" asked Bonnie, squinting in the same direction.

"Our leopard?" asked Donahue hopefully.

I shook my head. "Not likely."

"Why not?"

"No cover," I pointed out. "It's a steep slope, but leopards hide up trees, not down rocks, and that slope's never held a tree in its life. Besides, most of the vegetation colonized here after the snow left; the stuff that was here a century ago couldn't have supported enough prey animals."

"You're sure?"

"This is my specialty," I replied. "It's why you brought me along."

Muro turned to Gorman with a triumphant smile on his narrow face. "*Chui!*" he exclaimed.

"Chewy?" asked Ray. "Sounds like he's talking about gum."

"*Chui,*" I repeated. "It's the Swahili word for leopard."

"I thought you said it couldn't be a leopard," said Donahue.

"I said it wasn't likely," I replied. "And it wasn't." I began trudging off in the direction Muro had indicated. "Let's go take a look at it."

Muro rushed past me and actually trotted the remaining half mile, then began yelling something in Chagga that even Gorman couldn't understand.

We all hurried forward, panting for breath, ignoring the cold and the sharp pains in our chests, and a few minutes later we had gathered around a mound of dirt-covered slush. There was obviously a body under it. One leg stuck out, rigid and frozen, covered with a brown pelt.

"That sure as hell doesn't look like a leopard's leg to me," said Bonnie.

"It isn't," I said.

"I agree," said Gorman. "That foot never held claws, retractable or otherwise."

"Is it a human?" asked Ray.

It was so obviously *not* a human that no one even bothered answering him.

"Well, let's pull it out and see what we've got," said Bonnie.

"It is the property of the Tanzanian government," said Njobo. "Nobody may touch it."

"I agree," I said. "No one lays a finger on it. Our DNA and any stray microbes that we're carrying could contaminate it. I need to send for the proper equipment to move it to a secure environment."

"No one is moving it anywhere," insisted Njobo.

"I'm not talking about moving it off the mountain," I assured him. "But we need to move it to a place where a crew of experts can examine it.

There must be a secure cave higher up, where it's still freezing."

"It stays where it is."

"Do you really want to be known as the man who was responsible for screwing up the first example of whatever it is?" I asked. "What will your superiors say?"

Njobo was silent for a moment. "I will consider it," he said at last. Then he added: "If anyone touches it without my permission, I will send them back down the mountain alone."

Gorman stared at the thing. "I thought I knew every animal that ever lived on Kilimanjaro, but I sure don't recognize this one," he said. He turned to Muro. "Have a couple of the porters come up and shovel some of this junk off it." He paused and looked at Njobo. "With your permission," he added.

Njobo looked questioningly at me.

I nodded. *"Carefully,"* I said.

Muro relayed the order, and twenty minutes later two of the porters had meticulously uncovered the whole body. It looked bipedal, maybe sixty inches top to bottom. It was definitely not human or anthropoid, and I couldn't think of any other bipedal animals that large. It didn't quite have a snout, but its face seemed somehow elongated. It's fur – down, really – was auburn, and nowhere near as thick as an ape's.

"Well, Professor?" said Gorman. "I admit I'm stumped."

"Jim, Bonnie," I said, "take all the pictures you can of it. Take it from every angle. Take close-ups of every feature. When you're done, I want to transfer them to my computer and e-mail them to some of my colleagues."

"Just what kind of animal is it?" asked Bonnie.

"I don't want to offer an opinion until I consult with the men I'm sending the photos to," I answered.

"A missing link?" asked Ray.

I shook my head. "We never evolved from *that*," I said. "Look at it. The eyes are set lower in the head than the nostrils. Its hips aren't jointed like any human or ape I've ever seen. And its got opposing thumbs." I paused and considered that. "I've never seen *anything* with opposing thumbs." I kept cataloging the differences. "From the structure of the jaw and the few teeth I can see, I'd guess it's an omnivore."

"Intelligent?" asked Bonnie.

"It's possible," I replied. "It's got a big enough brain pan."

"But it's not wearing any clothes or trinkets," said Ray.

"Not all men wore clothes or trinkets," I said. "At least, not until they ran into other men who had better preachers or better weapons."

Donahue let out a whoop, and we all turned to look at him.

"A genuine Man from Mars!" he hollered happily. "We're all going to be millionaires — the first expedition ever to discover one!"

"We don't know *what* it is yet," I pointed out. "This thing is going to require a *lot* of study. Tonight I'll contact some of my colleagues and urge them to come over here to examine it. Then I have to find some people who know what they're doing and have the proper equipment to move it to a secure cave."

"You know," said Bonnie thoughtfully, "we've got a better mystery on our hands than Papa ever did. All he had to figure out was what a leopard was doing above the snow line. *We* have to figure out what this *is* as well as what it was doing here."

They guessed at its origins and talked and took their pictures, but I could tell that each of them was thinking the same thing:

Could it be, could it possibly be an alien? And if so, what was it doing on Earth. Why was nobody aware of it before today? And more to the point, why was it buried above the snow line on mighty Kilimanjaro?

Jim Donahue walked up to the body, bent over it, and began photographing it in small sections, taking more than one hundred photos before he'd captured every square inch of it. He photographed the foreface and took close-ups of the nostrils. He got on his knees, bent over, and photographed the hands and fingers. He was equally thorough on every part of the body. And then, when the party was getting a little bored and a little less attentive, he took four more quick photos of the almost imperceptible thing he had noticed on the left ankle.

He would get rich from the photos, of course, but he might get even richer when he sold an exclusive article explaining what the alien was doing here. Even if someone else in the party saw the slight abrasions on that left leg, they hadn't photographed men with similar abrasions. Men in custody.

Men in chains.

Convicts...

Jim Donahue was the first blind man.

WHAT THE PHOTOGRAPHER SAW

Earth hadn't been his first choice. The oxygen content was too high, the gravity too heavy, but his options had been limited. He had killed the guards as they were preparing to transport him to the high-security prison on Bareimus, where he would be one of only sixty-three living beings in the entire system. The prison was completely automated. The food was prepared by machines that had no motive power and never left the kitchen. There were no bars, just a trio of deadly force fields surrounding each cell, one always active and two in constant readiness in case the first ever failed. There would be no visitors, no exercise, no guards, no religious services, no medics – just sixty-three prisoners who would remain there until the last of them was dead.

He knew he would never be able to escape from Bareimus. The prison had been in existence for 364 years and there had never been a single escape. Gangs, indeed armies, had tried to break in to free their compatriots; none had succeeded and precious few had survived the single landing field's automatic and deadly defenses, programmed to destroy anything but the prison transport ship. So if he was ever to escape, it would have to be before he was delivered to the prison.

He couldn't wait until the ship to Bareimus took off. Even though there would be a pair of guards, there was no pilot. The ship was programmed to land at the prison, and even if he killed the guards there was no way to alter the ship's programming. It cost him half of his accumulated and ill-gotten gains, but he had a confederate kill one guard while he disabled the other as they walked to their ship at the spaceport.

His legs were still shackled, and the guards were past giving him the codes that would unlock them, so he took a pulse gun from one of them and blew the chains apart. He'd worry about removing what remained from his legs later; at least now he had freedom of movement again.

His race disdained clothing, so he carried the pulse gun in his left hand and raced to the nearest small ship. There were shots from the command center. His confederate screamed and fell to the ground, spurting blood, but he made it to the ship unscathed. A figure stood in the hatch, telling him not to come any closer. He fired the gun before the ship's owner finished his warning, stood aside as the body tumbled down to the ground, raced into the ship, and ordered the hatch to close and lock behind him.

It took him less than thirty seconds to break the ship's security code. (That was, after all, his specialty.) The ship asked for his name. He knew he couldn't use his real name, that any ship on the planet would shut down all systems the instant he uttered it, so he thought back to his childhood and used the name of a youthful friend, one he hadn't seen in twenty years.

"My name," he said, "is Machti."

"Destination?"

He looked at the viewscreen and saw that the security guards would reach him in about thirty seconds.

"What's the nearest world with an oxygen content similar to ours?"

"Define similar," said the ship.

"Within ten percent."

"The third planet in the Sol system."

"Take off immediately."

The ship made no verbal response, but he could feel the gravitational force as it shot up to the stratosphere and then beyond.

"Do you have any of the planet's languages in your data bank?" he asked as the ship began approaching light speeds.

"No. I have never been there."

"But you knew the oxygen content," said the being that was now Machti.

"The atmospheric content *is* in my data bank; the native languages are not," said the ship. "It is entirely possible that no ship has ever landed there." While Machti was considering that answer, the ship announced that they were being pursued.

"Wonderful," muttered Machti. "By how many ships?"

"Two."

"Can they overtake us?"

"Eventually."

"Before we reach Sol's system?"

"No."

"All right," said Machti. "We'll land there, and I'll stay in hiding for as long as it takes for them to forget about me or at least decide I'm not worth the trouble, and then we'll find a more hospitable world." He paused. "How long will it take to get there?"

"Through normal space, seven years and—"

"*Not* through normal space," he interrupted.

"Via the Jaxtoplin Wormhole, three days."

"Go that way."

"That is three of *our* days," continued the ship. "Based on the destination world's rotation speed, it will be 3.4983 of their days."

"Just do it!" snapped Machti.

The ship headed for the wormole, and Machti spent the next hour experimenting with the remains of the shackles until he found the code that unlocked the right one. Try as he might, he couldn't make the one on his left leg open; the chip had been damaged when he'd destroyed the chain. He explored the small interior of the ship, found a laser pistol, and turned it on his shackle. The shackle became hotter and hotter still. He screamed in pain, but kept the laser trained on it, weakening its structure. He finally was able to pry it off with one of the galley's eating tools.

He limped to the ship's medical stores, found some ointments to rub on his ankle, and spent the next fifteen hours sleeping. When he awoke he found out that the police ships were still in hot pursuit and had entered the wormhole only a minute or two after his own ship.

"Go faster!" he ordered.

"Speed is meaningless inside a wormhole, where the laws of the universe do not apply," responded the ship.

"Can they catch us?"

"Not unless the wormhole wishes them to."

"Wormholes don't think or wish," said Machti irritably.

"My conceptual vocabulary is limited," replied the ship. "There is no reason to assume they can catch us within the wormhole. Similarly, there is no reason for them *not* to catch us in a timeless and spaceless area outside the universe."

"Will you know if they are getting close to us?"

"Define 'close'," said the ship.

"Within firing range?"

"If you will tell me what weapons you are theorizing, I can answer the question."

"Your own weapons!" snapped Machti.

"I am not equipped with any weaponry," said the ship.

"What good are you?" growled Machti. Then: "Don't answer that question."

He spent the rest of the voyage studying what little was known of his destination's geography, medicating his ankle, and catching up on his sleep.

The ship woke him from his latest slumber with an announcement: "We have emerged from the wormhole, we are in Sol's system, we are approaching the third planet, and I need landing coordinates."

"How far behind are the two police ships?" demanded Machti. "In minutes, not distances."

"Three and fourteen minutes."

"I thought they went into the hole together."

"Clearly I will again have to explain the absence of the known laws of the universe inside a wormhole," said the ship.

"Don't bother," said Machti.

"The coordinates, please?" insisted the ship, producing a holographic display of Earth rotating slowly on its axis.

"Longitude and latitude? I don't know them." Machti pointed toward Africa. "This seems to be the least-populated continent, except for the ice- covered one. At least it has the fewest signs of civilization." Since he had neither asked a question nor issued a command, the ship remained silent. "Three minutes, you say?"

"2.9376 minutes, to be exact."

"Let me think," said Machti. "If you put me down in a city, there will be no way to keep my presence a secret, and the subsequent excitement will alert my pursuers to where I am. And if you set me down on a flat plain, they'll pinpoint your location, scan the limits of where I could get to in three minutes, spot me with their sensors, and that will be the end of it." He studied the globe again, and suddenly his eyes narrowed. "I'm getting an idea. Where is the tallest mountain on the continent?"

"Right here," said the ship, and Kilimanjaro began flashing brightly on the holographic globe.

"All right," said Machti. "If I were to jump out of the hatch while you flew directly over it, have we anything aboard that could break or ease my fall?"

"Yes."

"All right, here's what we'll do. Enter the atmosphere almost directly over the mountain, swoop down toward it, open your hatch, and I'll jump out. The odds are that they won't see me, and if you don't slow down they'll have no reason to assume I'm not still aboard you. Then go to the southern end of the continent, land in a barren field for thirty seconds, and then take off and fly back to your point of origin. They'll assume I got off there, and will spend their time searching the area for me. When they realize it's fruitless, they'll return home as well." He looked around the small ship. "Where is it?"

"Where is what?"

"Whatever I'm going to use to break my fall." The top of a bulkhead slid open, revealing a small parachute. "You're sure this will work? It doesn't look very substantial."

"It has been field-tested."

"All right. I'm in no position to argue. How far behind is the nearer ship now – rounded off to seconds?"

"Two minutes and fifty-eight seconds."

"Just make sure you stay ahead of it."

"It cannot catch me unless I malfunction," replied the ship.

Machti said nothing more until they entered Earth's atmosphere. Then he walked to the hatch.

"How soon do we reach the mountain?" he asked.

"Approximately four minutes," answered the ship.

"Get as low over it as you can and then open the hatch."

Machti waited impatiently until the ship made its approach and leveled out. After what seemed an eternity to him the hatch slid open and he dove out through it. The parachute computed his weight, sensed the approach of the mountain, and opened just in time to prevent him from suffering any serious injury.

He touched down on an icy slope, rolled over twice, and began sliding down the slope until his descent was blocked by large icy ledge. He looked up, but could see neither his ship nor the two pursuers.

He climbed out of the chute and buried it in the snow, then surveyed his surroundings. He was within a thousand feet of the mountaintop, and perhaps eighteen thousand feet above the savanna. Down the sides of the mountain he could see heavily-forested slopes, and below that a river and even a village of mud-and-straw huts.

And then he saw it: the police ship, hovering just above Kilimanjaro. He couldn't spot its companion. Possibly he'd fooled one of them, possibly it simply hadn't arrived yet. But at least one of them hadn't fallen for his ruse.

He hid in the shadow of a large rock, hoping that the ship would decide it had been mistaken and take up pursuit of his empty ship, but instead it just stayed there, and he realized its scanners were seeking out life forms from his planet. They were looking for him, and his readings would be like no other.

He knew the ship couldn't stay there long without being noticed, and since this planet hadn't yet developed spaceflight, they wouldn't want to be spotted and either questioned or, more likely, fired upon. All he had to do was stay hidden for another hour at most, probably just a few minutes...

He heard the growl before he spotted the source of it: a lone leopard about fifty yards away. It approached him slowly, and he stood up and faced it. Another growl from the leopard was matched by his own growl. That seemed to startle and unnerve the leopard; its prey wasn't supposed to growl back.

They stared at each other for a long minute, alien and leopard, and finally the leopard turned and began slinking back down the mountain, off the snow cap and toward the lush forest below.

Machti breathed a sigh of relief and looked up. The ship was still there. It obviously hadn't pinpointed him yet, because it possessed weapons that could take off the top thousand feet of the mountain or home in on a tiny target a mile away. He remained sheltered and hidden by the outcropping, certain that the ship would be leaving soon – but it didn't, and suddenly he realized the true situation. This was a primitive planet, and he was, by choice, on the most primitive part of it. Not only didn't they have spaceflight, they didn't have sensors – or if they did, they had them in the cities, not on this mountain that seemed to house only wild animals and a few people living in huts. And that meant the ship could hover there for weeks, maybe months, before anyone spotted it.

He spent the night under the outcropping, hopeful that the furry pelt that covered him would protect him from the cold – and for a few hours it did. But by morning he was freezing, and he decided that he would have to descend below the snow line if he was to survive.

He began walking gingerly, careful of the ice and the hidden rocks beneath the snow…and suddenly the energy pulse from the ship]s cannon missed him by less than ten feet. He began racing toward safety – a huge mound of snow that probably covered an equally large rock – but another burst of energy demolished the mound before he could reach it.

Machti looked down the mountain. The snow and ice were too steep. He knew he could never race down the slope at any speed; he'd surely slip and fall first, and if he fell hard enough, or fell the wrong way and broke something, he'd be a perfect target for the police ship. He turned and began retracing his steps. The higher he went, the more outcroppings there were to afford him cover, and soon he was back as high as when the ship had first seen him.

The firing stopped. Primitive as this world's inhabitants were, the officers clearly thought that if they fired their weapons enough, *somebody* would see it and report it. The ship hovered some two hundred feet above the snowy surface, its crew content to wait until Machti was compelled to leave to find food.

Machti stayed under the outcropping until three hours after the sun had set. Then he ventured forth again, only to be shot at instantly. He cursed himself for not realizing that the officers didn't have to see him, that their weapons could home in on his motion or even his body heat. He took up his position under the outcrop again and decided he had no choice but to outwait the ship.

By midmorning he decided to take a quick look and see if it was still hovering – and found that his feet and joints had frozen, that he was almost incapable of motion.

Now he began panicking. He'd been almost two days without food, he was on a freezing mountaintop, and he couldn't move. He forced himself to stand up, then painfully moved one foot ahead of the other. The outcrop was almost twenty feet long, so he had room to take a few steps while still protected, then turn and walk back, and continue doing it until some of his range of motion returned.

He took a step, leaning a hand against the outcrop for support, then another, then a third – and then his foot slipped on the ice, he fell heavily, and began sliding down the snow. He expected the ship to fire on him at any second, but either they hadn't noticed, or more likely had decided he was never going to get up under his own power again.

Fifty feet he slid, then eighty, then a hundred and forty. Finally the ground – or at least the snow – leveled out, and he came to rest. He tried to get up and found that he couldn't. He tried to crawl toward another outcrop, and couldn't manage that either. He became vaguely aware that it was starting to snow again. He lay on his back, staring up at the alien sun, wishing he could feel its life-giving warmth, and suddenly a smile crossed his face.

At least, he thought, *you won't be taking me to Bareimus. The snow will cover me completely in another few minutes, and I will lay here on this strange world and this inhospitable mountain for all eternity. Or perhaps some day in the far future one of the hut dwellers' descendants will find what's left of me, and try to convince his friends that this planet had been visited by an alien… and they will laugh and tease and humiliate him so much that he'll cover me back up and never mention me again.*

2038 A.D.

Bonnie stared down at the body. "Was he a meat-eater, do you think?"

"I'll have to examine his teeth," I said. "And one of my colleagues will examine the contents of his stomach."

"Provided he didn't starve to death," said Ray Glover.

"Even if he did, there will be traces," I said.

"He doesn't look particularly shaggy," continued Ray. "And if he's been up here any length of time, he'd have been in the middle of the glacier, not the lower edge of it. If he wasn't hunting, what the hell was he doing here? I mean, this couldn't have been his natural habitat, could it?"

Gorman chuckled at that. "Men have been climbing Kilimanjaro for hundreds of years," he said. "Maybe thousands. No one's ever seen one of these before, so I think you're safe in saying it's not his natural habitat. I think the main questions are: what is he, and what was he doing up here?"

"That's what we hope to find out," I said.

Jim Donahue patted his camera lovingly. "Whatever it is, we're the first to find it, and I'm the first to photograph it."

"Probably," I agreed.

"What do you mean *probably*?" he repeated. "The damned thing's been buried in the ice since it died. No one's ever seen it before."

Charles Njobo stared at the body of the creature. He knew this party was not the first to discover it, because there were no weapons to be found anywhere in the vicinity of the body. He could believe that the creature's clothes had rotted away over the years despite the snow and ice, but not its weapons. Someone had taken them,

Why was he so certain? Because he was a Zanake, and because he was a Tanzanian. Before there was a Tanzania, there were just tribes – and the Zanake had been exploited by the Arabs and then the Germans and the British, and been conquered by the Maasai, and the Nandi and half a dozen other tribes. Then they became Tanzanians, and the Kenyans had dominated them economically, and Idi Amin's Uganda had invaded them, and the great powers in Europe still held their purse strings. So of course the creature was an alien, here to conquer his people. Wasn't that what everyone came here for?

Charles Njobo was the second blind man.

WHAT THE GOVERNMENT OFFICIAL SAW

His name was Zhond Matoka, and this was his continent. Which is say, it was the continent he was responsible for. Other land masses had other members of his race scouting them out, probing for weaknesses, mapping the population centers, estimating the defense capabilities. But Africa, as the inhabitants called it, was his.

He was at first confused at the physical variety of the sentient beings, because on his own world, and almost all the worlds he had scouted for the military, when there were minor variations – skin color, number of limbs, skin texture, whatever – one race had proven dominant and eliminated the competing races. It was, to Matoka, the natural order of things. Yet here, while the dominant variety or species was black, there were reds and browns, a handful of golds, and one type that ranged from pink to tan, all living on the same land. It went against his experience, and he decided he would have to learn more about this race that alternately called itself man or human before he was ready to report back to the mother ship.

He had spent a week in Egypt, going forth only at night, swathed in Arab robes and a turban. He was awed as any tourist by the pyramids and the ruins of Karnak and Luxor. Yet try as he might, he could find no sign of the race that required those massive doorways, or sat on those gigantic thrones. He went as far as Abu Simbel, with its 60-foot-high representations of Rameses II and it's almost equally large statues of Nefertari, and finally concluded that this race of giants had either died off, or had left the Earth to settle (or conquer) another planet. Given their size, it was inconceivable to him that they had been defeated by the comparatively tiny species that now inhabited the continent.

He'd followed the Nile all the way down to Uganda, then left it and began observing the cities, analyzing their weaponry. Kampala presented no threat to the invading force, and he contacted the mother ship, asking where they wanted him to go next. They didn't have the names of the cities or countries, but they could pinpoint the artificial structures and measure the neutrino activity, and based on this they could direct him to those cities that seemed the most able to defend themselves against a concerted attack.

From Kampala they directed him east, over Mount Elgon and past the vast Rift Valley, to Nairobi. As he had done with the other cities he'd explored, he remained in hiding during the daylight and emerged only after midnight, when most of the city was asleep and those who weren't could plausibly be divided into miscreants and police officers.

He found a drunk sleeping in an alley and relieved him of his tribal robe, wrapping it around himself. He had seen other men wearing hats and turbans, and wished this one had one, but he settled for what he could get. The tallest building, towering above all others, was the recently-constructed Kenyatta Conference Center, begun in 1966 and not completed until 1973. He examined it as thoroughly as he could without entering it, but was unable to find any trace of its sensing devices, its radar trackers, or its cannons – yet he *knew* they must be there. War was the natural state for sentient beings, and surely this building would be the greatest prize a conquering army could claim.

He was so intent on finding the Center's hidden defenses and weaponry that he didn't see the two uniformed men coming out of the Long Bar of the New Stanley Hotel a block away from where he lurked in the shadows.

"What the hell is *that?*" said one of the men.

Matoka turned, saw the men, and froze momentarily.

"Jesus!" said the other. "That better be what men look like when you've had too much to drink."

"That's no man!"

"I was afraid you were going to say that."

"Draw your gun and let's find out what it is," said the first man, withdrawing his own handgun from its holster.

When the men didn't shoot, Matoka realized that they were only displaying their guns to frighten or impress him, or at best for self-protection. He knew he could kill them both before they could get off a shot, but he also knew that if he did so, the inhabitants would realize they were up against a race with superior weaponry. He doubted that they had anything that could counteract his weapon, but he had no intention of using it against two inebriated men and being proven wrong.

He ducked behind a nearby building, and the two men broke into a run. He could hear them coming, looked around for a doorway, couldn't see any that were clearly unlocked – and he couldn't take the chance that the door he went to wouldn't open – so at the last instant he dove into a huge metal dumpster. It must have belonged to a restaurant, because it was filled with loosely-tied plastic bags of partially-eaten human food. The odor was sick-making, but he held perfectly still as he heard the two men race up, come to a stop, and begin speaking.

"Where the hell did he go?" asked one.

"Maybe he never was," suggested the other hopefully.

"I saw him. You saw him. We couldn't both have the same delusion."

"Maybe we didn't. What color was yours?"

"Dark gray, maybe."

"Mine was brown."

"Dark gray and brown can look at lot alike from a distance at two in the morning."

"How many legs?"

"Two arms, two legs, just like us."

"What was he wearing?"

"I don't know. By the time I got a clear look at him, he was running hell for leather for this alley." A pause. "So what do we do now? If we report it, we're going to spend a lot of time with the shrink, and if he doesn't believe us, and there's no reason why he should, we could be looking at brig time."

"I know," said his companion. "I suppose we could just forget it. It's not as if he threatened us."

"Then it's settled?"

"Yeah, it's settled."

The two men began walking back toward the New Stanley. "What do you suppose it was, really?"

"I don't know."

"A chimpanzee, maybe, or a gorilla?"

"Wearing clothes?" said his companion with a laugh. "It'd be the first of either that was even seen in Kenya, let alone Nairobi. Besides, what would a chimp or a gorilla be doing in Nairobi?"

"Yeah, it's probably better that we decide here and now that we never saw anything."

Then they were out of earshot. Matoka waited another five minutes to be sure they didn't come back, then climbed out of the dumpster. Despite the plastic bags, he found himself wiping pieces of lettuce and some orange peels off himself.

He began walking south until he'd passed out of the commercial sector and found himself in a dilapidated area of poorly-constructed dwellings. He stood in an alley between two rows of shanties in desperate need of repair, and pressed one of his thumbs against the chip that had been embedded in his neck.

"Yes?" said a voice inside his head.

"I regret to report that I was seen tonight."

"That is not good, Zhond Matoka," said the voiceless voice from the mother ship.

"I require instructions," said Matoka. "I am in a city of perhaps six million. The two men who saw me have decided not to report the incident. Shall I remain here?"

"No."

"Where shall I go next?"

"There is a large city a little more than 400 miles south of you. And since you started at the north end of the continent, it makes sense to keep moving south."

"Understood and acknowledged," said Matoka, ending the pressure on the chip and breaking the connection.

He began walking south again. A few people saw him, or at least saw his outline, but it was very dark, and the people who lived in these slums were not inclined to call the authorities for any reason. About an hour later he came upon a bicycle that was not locked and chained, and after a moment's hesitation – he had never ridden one, though he'd watched others – he appropriated it. Areas like this, he knew, did not report theft any more than they reported strangers wandering the streets in the middle of the night. The owner would probably just go out and steal another.

He knew that he couldn't ride along the roads or anywhere near them, not in the daylight, and he couldn't make much progress riding it over bumpy and frequently-fenced fields, so he abandoned it when he reached the southernmost end of town an hour before daylight.

He looked around, and saw a large building with a number of trucks backed up to it. He approached it carefully and studied it. It seemed to be a factory of some kind, but he couldn't tell what it manufactured because all he could see from his vantage point was the shipping dock, filled with hundreds of huge wooden and cardboard boxes.

The backs of the trucks were open. One old man operated a forklift, loading the boxes into the trucks. There was no one else to be seen. Matoka's problem was how to determine which of the trucks would be going south, and finally he figured it out. Each of the trucks bore license plates. There were sixteen trucks. Thirteen had license plates of one type or color. Two more had a second color, and a single one had a third.

Logic dictated that the thirteen trucks were all from Nairobi, or at least from Nairobi's country, which was spelled Ke-n-y-a. Nairobi was in the southern part of the country, so it was likely (but not certain) that the two trucks with similar plates belonged to the adjacent southern country, and the other one to a country to the north or west.

He looked at the sky. It would be light in another half hour, at least light enough that he couldn't climb into one of the trucks unseen, so he approached them, waited patiently until the forklift driver was busy loading boxes into a truck thirteen vehicles removed from the one he'd chosen, and he quickly climbed into it. He moved some of the boxes to leave himself room to sit and even lie down if it was an exceptionally long or wearing trip, made sure that no one standing behind the truck could spot him, and settled in for the ride.

As if on cue, the driver arrived at sunrise, closed the back of the truck, climbed into the driver's seat, and began speeding down the road. The whole time the truck was in motion Matoka was considering all his alternatives for when the truck stopped, because he was only hidden from view as long as the boxes remained where they were.

The truck slowed and came to a stop in two hours, but no one opened the back, and it began moving again in twenty minutes. Matoka couldn't know it, of course, but it had merely stopped for the border crossing into Tanzania.

An hour later it stopped again, this time in the city of Arusha. Matoka huddled in a corner, his weapon in his hand, wishing now that he'd made the journey on foot, walking by night, hiding and sleeping by day. It was too late to concern himself with that, though, because the back of the truck was being opened.

"What have you got for us?" asked a voice.

"Two couches and five chairs," answered the driver. "It's right here on the manifest."

"What about the brass lamp?"

"I don't know anything about a lamp," said the driver.

"Well, come on in while I call your boss and find out what happened to it. Then if you're hungry we can grab some lunch, and we'll unload the cargo after that."

"Sounds good to me," said the driver, and Matoka could hear the two of them walking away. He waited a few minutes, then cautiously stuck his head out the back. No one was around, and he quickly climbed out of the truck and hid behind a small shanty. He felt exposed there, and when the coast was clear he raced across the dirt road to an empty field filled with waist-high grasses, lay down on his belly, and waited for dark.

When night fell he contacted the ship again, to report his progress.

"Stay hidden for a few days," said the voice that seemed to originate within his head. "The situation may be changing."

"In what way?" asked Matoka.

"I don't know. I just know we've been told to suspend all operations and await further orders."

"When shall I check in with you again?"

"Three days."

The communication ended, and Matoka surveyed his surroundings. Towering above everything, filling the horizon, its snowcap shining in the moonlight, was Kilimanjaro. He couldn't make out any of the features except the snow, but he knew from the brief glance he'd had when he left the truck that its slopes were heavily forested, which implied that he would be able to remain hidden there for as long as need be. He assumed there would be some towns or villages, but it wouldn't take much to avoid them on a gigantic mountain like this one.

He began approaching it, hastening his stride so he could reach the forests at the base of it before sunrise, and indeed he reached his destination with almost an hour to spare. He moved away from the road, which he was sure would pass through a number of villages on its ascent, and instead stayed in the dense forest, moving up the slope at a far more leisurely pace.

After he'd ascended some three thousand feet he heard a low growl, and turned to find himself facing a lion. Most of its mane was missing, torn out by constantly brushing against thornbushes, and it bore several scars on its body. There was a hint of a limp, and although Matoka knew nothing of lions, he knew that this one was too infirm to hunt whatever was its normal prey, and had chosen to hunt anything it could find – including men – in the forest.

Matoka slowly drew his weapon. He didn't want to use it if he didn't have to. Not only was he trying to save his ammunition, but he didn't want anyone examining the lion's corpse and finding out that it had been killed by an unknown weapon. He backed away slowly, the lion approached slowly, and then the huge cat roared and charged. Matoka pressed the firing mechanism, and the lion was dead in mid-leap.

Matoka considered pulling the corpse to an outcrop and hiding it there, but the cat weighed close to five hundred pounds and he realized that moving it, especially on this terrain, was beyond his capabilities, so he left it where it lay and began ascending the mountain again, determined to put a few thousand feet between himself and the cat's corpse, just in case some man should discover it before the various scavengers had eaten enough of it to obliterate the reason for its death.

At six thousand feet he was charged by a rhino, and a leopard almost caught him at eight thousand feet. It was clear to him that the forest held too many dangers, that he would be safer moving higher up the mountain.

He had a scrape with a lone bull elephant at eleven thousand feet, but thereafter nothing attacked him, though he saw leopard signs up to just below the snow.

On the evening of his third day on Kilimanjaro, as he wandered the barren slopes just below the snow line clutching his now-tattered robe about him, he pressed a thumb against the chip in his neck and raised the mother ship again.

"This is Matoka," he said.

"I know who you are," came the reply. "Are you still in hiding?"

"Yes. But I am running low on ammunition, and such native foods as I can metabolize grow at a lower altitude on the mountain, where I am more likely to be seen. When can I either continue my trek to the south, or return to the mother ship?"

"We don't know."

"What is the problem?"

"The situation is unclear," replied the voice. "Evidently our colonies on Malpur and Samangiare are under attack. They should be able to defend themselves without recalling ships such as this one, but until we know for a fact that they won't require our presence, we have been ordered to hold our position."

"When shall I contact you again?"

"In five days."

"Five days?" he exclaimed.

"If there's any news before then, we will contact you."

"Make sure you do. I am cold and hungry, and I have very little ammunition left."

The connection ended, and Matoka found himself staring at a leopard his voice had attracted. He knew he could only activate his weapon three or four more times, so he chose to remain perfectly motionless. He didn't smell like anything the leopard had ever eaten or hunted, and he hoped that would discourage the cat – but there wasn't much for a carnivore to kill and eat this high on the mountain, and finally the leopard began approaching him. He reached for his weapon, his sudden movement precipitated a charge, and he barely killed the leopard before it could reach him.

During the next two days, he killed two more leopards, and realized that he was now totally out of ammunition. He tried eating the leaves and the bark from a variety of trees, but couldn't metabolize them. Sick and weak, he realized that he couldn't defend himself should he be attacked by yet another predator, so he climbed onto the snow cap.

He didn't think he could last three more days, so he tried to contact the ship. All he got was a recorded message: "We will contact you when there is a change in status. There is a possibility we are being monitored, whether by Earth or by the enemy. Do not break radio silence again."

The connection was broken. He looked up the ice cap. There had to be some caves up there, someplace to get away from the awful cold. Maybe he could find something edible. Here and there a tree or bush broke through the snow cover. Maybe he could metabolize one of them.

And maybe not. He looked longingly down at the forest he had been so anxious to leave. Maybe he didn't have a weapon, but he could climb trees for safety. He tried to remember if leopards climbed trees.

He took a few steps down the ice cap. Then he looked ahead. There was a leopard standing there, right at the edge of the snow, glaring hungrily at him.

With a sigh he turned back and began ascending the snow cap again. There had to be caves up ahead, and right now he would put up with the hunger if he could just get out of the frigid wind.

He climbed for another hour, and found that he was too weak to continue. There might be caves up ahead, but he knew he would never see them. His only hope was the ship. He sat down in the snow, vaguely aware of the lack of feeling in his feet and legs, and pressed against the chip again.

This time there was no response at all, not even an order not to break radio silence.

His situation looked as bleak as the top of the mountain. He fought to stay awake, but felt consciousness slipping away.

"They will call," he muttered as he slowly toppled over onto his side. "I'm one of them. They won't leave me here." And as he closed his eyes for the last time, he whispered once more: "They will call."

2038 A.D.

"You're the expert," said Ray Glover, turning to me. "How long could it last up here on the mountain?"

"That depends," I said.

"Why can't scientists ever just give an answer without qualifications?" he grumbled.

"I don't know his lung capacity. I don't know what he ate. I don't know the oxygen content on his home planet. I don't know—"

"Never mind," he interrupted me.

"There's a much more interesting question anyway," said Adrian Gorman.

"Oh?" said Ray. "What?"

"Is he the only one on the mountain?" said Gorman.

"Damn!" said Bonnie excitedly. "You think there might be more?"

Gorman shrugged expansively. "Why not?"

Ray looked at me again. "I don't suppose you have an opinion?"

I shook my head. "Not without more data."

"You know," mused Gorman, "the ice was a lot farther down the mountain when Hemingway was here – well, when he was supposed to be here – and a lot farther down a few hundred years earlier. Who knows how long the alien's been up here? Maybe we just need to walk around where the glacier used to be."

"You won't find anything," I told him.

"Why not?"

"Scavengers," I said. "There are hyenas and jackals up here, as well as vultures and marabou storks. And even if there weren't, the ants would have it picked clean in a couple of days."

"I don't know," said Gorman. "This guy was at least partially exposed, and he's still here."

"You don't get ants in all this ice," I replied. "And he's still frozen. No odor to attract the scavengers until he starts thawing. Any lower down on the mountain and these conditions wouldn't exist."

Gorman shrugged. "Makes sense," he said. "Still, it was an idea. Is there some machine that can spot them through the snow and ice?"

"There is," I said.

"Maybe we should think of getting one. After we tell the world about this guy, I think whoever manufactures it would give us a few for free in exchange for our mentioning their names."

"You can try," said Jim Donahue, who'd been silent up to this point. "But I don't think you're going to find any others."

"Why not?" asked Gorman.

"I think he was a loner," said Donahue.

"Why?"

"Just a hunch," said Donahue, who then clammed up.

Gorman looked down at the alien and tried to recon-struct what it was doing on a mountain in the middle of nowhere, light years from its home, breathing air it was never meant to breathe, eating food it was never meant to eat. Whatever its reason for abandoning its home world, one thing he was sure of: it wouldn't have left alone. More likely it came for the same reason so many others had come to Africa: to colonize it. And that was clearly not the task for a solo visitor, so no mat-ter what Donahue and the others thought, this creature figured to be just one member of the landing party, one cog in a machine that hoped to settle here...

Adrian Gorman was the third blind man.

What the Guide Saw

The world of Pharachine had become intolerable. Overpopulated, under-managed, its natural resources plundered, its air polluted, the average citizen's life expectancy dropped every year. Finally the Pharachi had decided to colonize other worlds before it was too late.

They knew better than to put all their eggs in one basket, so they had chosen the twenty most likely worlds. The requirements were simple enough: they had to circle a type G star at distances of forty to one hundred million miles, they had to have an oxygen content of between fifteen and thirty-five percent, they had to have at least a two-to-one ratio of water to land, they had to have a protective layer in the atmosphere to negate the effects of the star's ultra-violet rays, and they had to be populated by life forms. Not necessarily sentient races, but by *something* which would act as proof that the worlds truly were habitable.

Nibolante and his family were in the fourteenth group, which was to colonize the third planet of a yellow star, clearly a type G, that was well out on one of the spiral arms of the galaxy. They packed those goods they could not do without, and were ensconced on the huge ship when it took off on the appointed day.

It would take just under four hundred days to reach the planet. During the voyage, there would be schooling not only for the children, but also for the colonists, teaching them a variety of survival methods until they could build and establish a thriving city. Enough neutrino activity had been observed that it was all but certain that the planet was populated by an industrialized civilization.

They had entered the planet's system, and Nibolante and Marbovi. his mate, were putting their two children through yet another exercise aboard a small landing craft when disaster struck. Something *large* collided with the ship, possibly a meteor, possibly a comet. Whatever it was, it blew a large hole in the hull, and air began rushing out. The ship lurched crazily, and an automated voice announced that the structure would disintegrate within thirty seconds.

Nibolante knew no one could reach his landing craft in that time. In fact, most of them had already died from shock or asphyxiation. He rushed to the controls, cast off from the ship, and dared a look back just in time to see it vanish while still beyond the orbit of the outermost planet

"That should have been *us*," said Marbovi.

"Just be glad that it wasn't," said Nibolante, trying to remember the lectures about how to pilot the craft in case of emergency, for which this surely qualified.

"What are we to do?" she persisted. "There are only the four of us."

"Our colony will be a little smaller than anticipated," answered Nibolante. "But we have no other option but to continue to our destination."

"I didn't bargain to be the mother of a new race," said Marbovi bitterly.

"It might not be so bad," he said. "They're sentient, and at least they haven't damaged *their* planet the way we damaged ours."

"Will there be anyone to play with?" asked Sallassine, his son.

"Eventually," replied Nibolante. "I am certain that most sentient races are ultimately rational and friendly."

"What does that mean?" asked Sallassine.

"It means I think you will find playmates before long."

"Me too?" asked his daughter hopefully.

He smiled reassuringly at her. "You too."

It took them three days to reach their destination, and they took up a high orbit, studying the world, trying to decide where to land. Nibolante and Marbovi were in the galley, eating, when Sallassine called out: "Come quickly!"

Both parents, certain that one of the children was sick, raced to the control room. Cheenapo, their daughter, was playing with a favorite toy, and Sallassine was sitting before a viewscreen.

"What is it?" demanded Nibolante.

"Look," said Sallassine, pointing to the screen.

Nibolante stared at the screen and frowned. The powerful camera showed a huge explosion on an island at the eastern end of the planet's largest body of water.

"An accident at some factory?" asked Marbovi, staring at the mushroom cloud..

Nibolante adjusted the controls and shook his head. "A war."

"Are you sure?"

"That was a nuclear bomb," he said. "And *this*" – he had the screen pinpoint it – "is the airship that delivered it."

"What kind of world *is* this?" she asked.

"I don't know," he said. "I truly don't know."

"Can we go back?"

"Not in this vessel," answered Nibolante. "We haven't the fuel or the air, and even if we did, the engine's not up to it. For better or worse we're stuck here."

"What are we do to then?"

"We'll stay in orbit and study them until we can make a decision."

By the time a second bomb was dropped three days later, they'd monitored enough transmissions to know that the two destroyed cities were called Hiroshima and Nagasaki, but they had no idea what had caused the war, only that it seemed to extend to almost every land mass on the world.

"We will land where there is the least chance of our encountering the native inhabitants," announced Nibolante after two more days.

"That would seem to be the southern polar cap," remarked Marbovi.

He began taking readings, and after another day decided that the southern ice cap was too inhospitable to life: the temperatures – and it was the middle of winter in the southern hemisphere – were too frigid even for his species, and until he knew how their metabolism could handle living on a diet of aquatic life and avians, he didn't want to chance landing there.

The northern cap, on the other hand, seem more accommodating. The temperatures would be tolerable, and there was a variety of animal life and vegetation. If they couldn't find sustenance there, they probably couldn't find it anywhere.

His decision made, Nibolante maneuvered the ship to a completely deserted area about ten degrees south of the pole. They landed, decided to use the ship for their home until they were sure they wanted to take up permanent residence at this remote spot, and began exploring their surroundings.

All went well for three days. They found that they could indeed metabolize the creatures that lived in the sea, and while the temperature was less than they were used to, they were able to tolerate it. The atmosphere presented more of a problem; the oxygen content was too high. The vessel had medications to neutralize the effects, but the supply wasn't endless.

On the fourth day Nibolante came face-to-face with a polar bear bent over the remains of a dead fish it had been eating. Clearly it was a carnivore or an omnivore, but Nibolante felt no apprehension, because whatever the bear was genetically programmed to eat, his race had to be excluded since there had never been a member of it on the planet until he had landed four days ago.

Somehow, that fact didn't bother the bear in the least, and it began approaching Nibolante, who backed away. The bear kept walking toward him, and Nibolante kept backing up, and finally the bear lost all patience, roared an ear-splitting roar, and charged, Nibolante turned and raced toward the ship, yelling to Marbovi and the children to get inside it and to close and lock the hatch the second he entered.

He made it by less than two seconds. The bear couldn't stop in time, and skidded painfully into the hatch, precipitating another roar.

"What was *that*?" asked Marbovi.

"*I* know," offered Sallassine. "It is called a bear."

"What does it eat?" asked Nibolante, gasping for breath.

"Everything," said Sallassine.

"How many bears are there?"

"I don't know. I only studied polar bears."

"Polar bears?" asked Nibolante.

"The white ones. They think there are more than one hundred thousand."

"All over the world?"

Sallassine shook his head. "Just in the north."

Nibolante and Marbovi exchanged looks. After a moment Nibolante activated the ship's video and looked at the viewscreen. The polar bear was laying down – not sleeping, just patiently waiting – outside the hatch.

He checked it every few hours. The bear was still there. By midnight he'd been joined by another, and by sunrise there were a total of five polar bears surrounding the ship.

"This is intolerable," announced Nibolante. "We clearly cannot live here. I don't want my children to go armed every time they leave the ship."

"It would have been *fun*!" protested Sallassine.

"Until you were eaten," replied Nibolante. "I must study the computer and decide where we will move to."

"Don't forget that there is a terrible war going on," said Marbovi.

"I know. For that reason I think we can eliminate the continents called Europe, Asia, Australia, and North America. And we cannot live on the southern polar cap. That leaves two land masses, Africa and South America. Now, they *were* fighting in the north of Africa, but the computer tells me that it has been resolved."

"Is *everyone* on this world warlike?" said Marbovi.

"*We* aren't, and I must find a place where we'll be safe." He studied the computer further. "South America seems free from this conflict, but it is populated by the same species as the rest of the world."

"Isn't Africa?" asked Marbovi.

"Yes, of course," answered Nibolante. "I doubt that either continent would welcome us, but I think I've found a place where we can be relatively safe."

"Where?"

"There is a mountain in Africa, the tallest on the continent. It is in a thinly populated area, relatively few people live on it, those who *do* live on it live primarily on the lower sections. It had a huge ice cap, which can be seen literally fifty miles away, and no one lives above the tree line." Suddenly he smiled. "And there are no polar bears."

"If it is a mountaintop, there are clearly no oceans," she said. "So what will we eat?"

"There are dozens of game species on the mountain, some huge, some tiny, most of them edible. And there are streams and rivers filled with fish. And avians everywhere."

"And these warlike beings are just going to let you walk right in and kill and eat *their* prey animals?" Marbovi said sarcastically.

"Not everyone is armed with nuclear weapons," answered Nibolante. "From what I can gather, the residents of the mountain, indeed of the entire area, are a pastoral people who hunt and defend themselves with spears and bows and arrows."

"They can kill you just as dead with a spear or an arrow."

He smiled, got up, walked to a bulkhead, touched a particular spot on it, and the top slid back. He reached in and withdrew a set of goggles.

"These enable me to see in the dark as easily as in the daylight," he said. "They have nothing similar, and there are some dangerous animals on the mountain. I will hunt at nights, while they sleep." He paused. "You look dubious."

"We are leaving here because there are dangerous animals, and now you want to move to where there are *more* dangerous animals."

"There is a difference," he said. "The polar bears live on fish and the very few mammals they can find up here. But on the mountain, there are literally tens of thousands of herbivores. It means, first, that there will be enough food for us, and second, that no carnivores will wait for us outside the ship simply because there are no other prey animals."

She made no further comment, and he instructed the ship to lay in a course for Kilimanjaro. The planet's inhabitants had developed a primitive form of radar, but he knew the ship would be able to avoid or deflect it. It reached the mountain in the middle of the night, hovered above the top while its sensors sought out a flat area halfway up the glacier, and then gently lowered itself until it came to rest on the snow.

Nibolante used the ship's sensors to make sure there were no life forms within half a mile, then donned his goggles and stepped out onto the snow and ice. He took a deep breath and was pleased to find the air was thinner and the oxygen count lower than at the north polar cap. He looked down the mountain and couldn't see any villages, which meant that they wouldn't be able to see him or the ship either. He could hear the trumpeting of an elephant and the roar of a lion, but they were far down the mountain.

He spent a few more moments walking around what he thought of as his new homesite, then re-entered the ship.

"You'll like it," he announced to his mate. "The air is delicious."

"Air has no taste," replied Marbovi.

"*This* air does," he said enthusiastically. "And it's not as cold. I doubt that we'll need any protective coverings at all."

"You can stop promoting it," she said. "We're here, for better or worse."

"For better," he said. "You'll see."

"I'll tell you what I won't see," said Marbovi. "I won't see any other

Pharachi except for you and the children." She frowned. "Now or ever."

"You're looking at this all wrong," said Nibolante. "We lived. We survived. We will become the parents of a new race on a new world."

"We are four Pharachi on a world where the inhabitants spend their time killing each other. Why do you think they'll accept us – and if they don't, how long do you think we can stay hidden on this mountain?"

"Look," he said. "I wish the mother ship hadn't been destroyed. I wish all our friends were here with us. I wish the inhabitants welcomed us with open arms. But we're here, we're alive, and we have to make the best of it."

"This is not what I wanted for my children."

"You can't always have everything you want," he said irritably.

They exchanged hostile glares, then went to opposite ends of the ship to sleep.

Nibolante was up early in the morning, and took Sallassine and Cheenapo outside to see their new surroundings. Marbovi remained in the ship.

"I have been studying the fauna on the computer," said Sallassine. "I can identify any that we see."

"Try *that*," said Nibolante, pointing to an avian that was riding the warm thermals a few hundred yards out from the mountain.

"That is a fish eagle," said the youngster proudly.

Suddenly Nibolante smiled.

"What is so funny?" asked Sallassine.

"I have to believe you," he replied. "I haven't studied them."

Sallassine identified two more avians, then stared down the mountain. "How far down may we go?"

"Until we explore it further and see exactly where the villages are, I don't want you going more than two hundred feet below the tree line," answered Nibolante. The youngster looked his disappointment, and Nibolante laid a hand on his shoulder. "When you are a little bigger, and we know the mountain a little better, you can accompany me some nights when I am hunting for food."

"Really?" asked Sallassine, his face glowing with excitement.

"Really."

"Can we go down to the tree line now?"

"Yes, as long as you both stay very near me."

They made their way down the glacier to the tree line, then stopped and observed their surroundings. Suddenly Cheenapo pounced on something, and held it up a moment later.

"What is it?" she asked.

"It is called a lizard," said Sallassine. "It eats insects, whatever they are." He stared at it. "They can't be very big, these insects." He stared at it more closely, then frowned. "It is a gecko lizard or a ugama lizard, but I cannot remember which."

Cheenapo turned to her father. "Can I keep it?"

Nibolante frowned. "Conditionally."

"What does that mean?"

"We must find out what insects are, and if they live on the glacier. If they don't, the lizard will starve if you take it back to the ship."

"Can we walk a little farther?" asked Sallassine.

"Just a little," said Nibolante.

They walked another few hundred yards, which put them only sixty feet lower in altitude. They couldn't see any wildlife, but they could hear the trumpeting of an elephant, the squawks of birds, even the bellow of a buffalo.

"I am going to like it here," said Sallassine.

"I'm glad *someone* does," said Nibolante.

They remained where they were for almost an hour, then retraced their steps and made it back to the ship by midafternoon.

Cheenapo played with her lizard while Sallassine found out from the computer that they would find no insects for it to eat on the glacier. She announced that she still wanted a pet, but she would find one that lived on the glacier, one that wouldn't suffer from a change in environments.

"She will be disappointed," Sallassine told his father when they were alone. "Nothing lives up here. Except us."

"Nothing *lives* up here," agreed Nibolante, "but perhaps I can get something to *visit* us."

"I do not understand."

"Every time I make a kill, I will leave a piece of meat out at the very same spot. It may go unnoticed the first few times, but eventually something will discover the meat, and once it does I think it will come back again and again for a free meal. It will be bigger than a lizard – it may be one of those eagles – so it will not be a pet, but at least she'll be able to see it."

"And when it comes, I will identify it," said Sallassine.

Nibolante went hunting that night, gently placing the lizard under a bush where it would be safe at least until morning. Using a silent weapon he killed a young bush pig at thirteen thousand feet, then spent the rest of the night carrying the carcass back up to the ship.

"What am I supposed to do with this?" said Marbovi when she awoke and found the pig.

"We will cut off the portions we want to eat," said Nibolante, "and I will put the rest in the disintegrator."

"All right," she said. "What parts do you want to eat?"

He stared at it. "I guess we'll have to figure it out by trial and error."

"You chose it. You killed it. You figure it out."

"What is the matter with you?" he demanded.

"I hate this place."

He sighed deeply. "I suppose we can look in South America."

"'This place' is Earth, not the mountain!" she snapped, walking away.

He found a cutting instrument, sliced off the haunches, cut off the visible fat, and put the rest of it in the disintegrator. He realized that he could freeze it just by putting it outside, but he didn't want to attract any predators. He knew they rarely came up onto the glacier, but he didn't know what kind of delicacy a bush pig might be.

When he was done he was covered with blood, as was the area in which he'd been working, and he made a mental note to bleed his prey in the future before cutting it into pieces.

That was their routine for the next twenty days. Nibolante went down the mountain at nights whenever they needed more food. He and the children spent the days exploring the glacier and the area just below the tree line. Once they saw a rhino, and another time a buffalo. Marbovi remained in the ship, unhappy and uncommunicative.

September 14, 1945 began like any other day. Nibolante arose and prepared breakfast for his family, then went outside. Sallassine was already out, and digging a hole at the base of a rocky outcropping.

"What are you doing?" asked Nibolante.

"Look!" said Sallassine excitedly. "In the dirt below the snow!"

Nibolante leaned over to see what his son was pointing at. "Ants!" continued Sallassine. "Ants are insects! Now Cheenapo can have her pet!"

"Yes," agreed Nibolante. "If you can keep uncovering insects, I suppose she can."

"Shall we find one today?"

"Why not?" agreed Nibolante.

He waited for the children to finish eating, then led them down past the tree line. They spent almost two hours looking for a lizard without finding one.

"Don't worry," Nibolante told his daughter. "If we don't find one soon, we'll try again tomorrow."

"Maybe we should split up and cover more ground," suggested Sallassine.

"I don't want you out of my sight," said Nibolante. "There are many predators on the mountain."

"They don't come this high."

"They do if they're hungry enough. Just stay within sight."

"All right," said Sallassine, heading off to his left.

Nibolante took his daughter by the hand and began looking for a lizard again, checking behind every rock and under every bush. Every few minutes he turned and made sure that Sallassine was still in his line of sight.

They'd been looking almost half an hour when he heard the scream. He turned and saw something small and black tearing at his son's torso with sharp claws, biting him on the neck and shoulder. He raced toward them, screaming as he ran, and the creature scurried off at a speed he knew he couldn't match. Nor did he want to. Sallassine was torn and bleeding, barely conscious.

"Don't move, don't try to talk," said Nibolante. "I have nothing with me that can stop the bleeding. We have medications in the ship. I'll carry you there."

"I was looking out for lions and leopards," whispered Sallassine.

"Be quiet. Don't waste your strength."

"It was a honey badger," said Sallassine just before he lost consciousness.

Nibolante carried Sallassine as fast as he dared, conscious of the fact that Cheenapo couldn't keep up with him if he increased his speed. By the time he reached the ship his son's breathing was barely discernable.

"Marbovi!" he yelled as he reached the hatch. "There's been an accident! Bring the medication kit!"

She was waiting for him when he entered and laid Sallassine on a counter. She didn't ask what had happened. She just took one look at the child and turned to Nibolante.

"He's dead," she said dully.

"He moaned just a minute ago."

"He's *dead*," she repeated. "He's not breathing."

Nibolante tried to discern a heartbeat, and couldn't.

"Will he stay dead?" asked Cheenapo.

"Yes," said Marbovi. "He is just the first. This planet will kill us all."

"He never saw it," said Nibolante miserably. "It was such a *small* animal."

"And *you* never saw it," said Marbovi. "The difference is that you were *supposed* to see it." She glared at him. "You and this planet have killed my child. Go outside until dinnertime. I don't want to look at you."

He was about to say something, thought better of it, and walked out onto the glacier, riddled with guilt. The moment he did so the hatch slammed shut behind him.

"Why bother?" he muttered. "I'm not coming right back in."

Even as the words left his mouth, he realized that she had activated the engine. He raced to the hatch, pounding on it.

"What are you doing?" he yelled.

Of course there was no answer. A moment later the ship took off, and somehow he knew it would never land again on Earth.

He looked across the glacier. His weapons were on the ship. So was any protection against the elements, should it get any colder. So were all the medications.

He considered walking down the mountain into one of the villages, but he was not prepared to die just yet, and his observations of the human race's goodwill were not encouraging. Not that it would make any difference. He was alone on an alien world, the last of his species on this particular colony.

Still, he wasn't prepared to die just yet, if only because Marbovi had doubtless been sure he would. He began walking across the ice, looking for shelter from the wind that had just sprung up, and wondered how many days he could last before he became his race's second victim on this alien mountain.

2038 A.D.

"I'm feeling kind of useless," said Ray Glover. "I mean, it's a fabulous discovery and we'll probably all get rich and maybe even famous, but the fact remains that I'm the sound man for a video of a corpse."

"You'll have more than enough work soon," said Bonnie. "We'll be interviewing everyone before we leave the mountain."

"I know," said Ray. "In the meantime I'll just concentrate on trying to catch my breath."

Charles Njobo walked over to me. "When do you plan to contact your experts on your laptop?"

"In a few minutes," I said. "The sooner I do it, the better."

"Do not do so until after I contact my government," he said.

I wasn't happy about it, but it was his country, so I had no choice.

Just then I noticed a snowflake floating down, then another and another. Within three minutes we were actually in a snowstorm. We could look down the mountain and see that it was raining two thousand feet below us. Then, almost as suddenly as it started, it stopped.

"Well, now you know how he stayed hidden all this time," said Jim Donahue, gesturing toward the creature, which had a fine covering of snow.

Muro approached Njobo and spoke to him in low tones. Finally Njobo nodded his head, and Muro walked away. He was back about five minutes later with a leafy branch he'd found. He walked over to the creature, squatted down next to it, and began carefully dusting the snow off the body and head.

Njobo glared at me as if he expected me to object, but that was probably the best and safest way to brush away the snow.

I saw one of the porters approaching the creature. He stopped and stared down at it for a moment, and then Muro saw him and ordered him to get back with the other porters.

"What was that all about?" I asked.

Gorman spoke to Muro in a language I didn't understand, and then turned to me. "Muro doesn't know that porter, and he doesn't want him messing with the body."

"How can he not know him?" asked Donahue. "Aren't they all from the same village?"

Gorman shook his head. "They're from the same tribe, not the same village. Muro spends most of his time as a headman on climbing parties, so it's not all that strange that he hasn't seen him before."

Ray Glover began swaying, and suddenly he sat down heavily on the snow.

"Are you all right?" asked Bonnie solicitously.

"Just a little dizzy and short of breath," he answered.

"Just sit still and don't exert yourself," said Gorman. "Altitude affects people differently."

Glover stared at the creature. "I wonder how *he* handled it?" he mused.

More to the point, thought Glover, why did he subject himself to it? We're all pretending that he might not be an alien, but clearly that's exactly what he was. What was it that kept him on this mountain, with a whole world to explore? Was he hiding? Was he a refugee? Or was there something on this mountain, more than anyplace else, that attracted him? The locals have made great progress, but they're still primitive by the rest of the world's standards. Did he have some plan to elevate them? What about them could have so fascinated him that he chose to remain in this hostile environment?

Ray Glover was the fourth blind man.

WHAT THE SOUND MAN SAW

His name was B'num B'narr, and he'd spent half his adult life in jails on his home world. He wasn't a thief or a killer, a swindler or a sadist. He was, according to his government, a rabble-rouser and an insurrectionist. By his own definition, he was a moral being cast into a thoroughly immoral world. By the judge's definition, he was incapable of modifying his behavior, and since the world of Grafipo did not believe in the death penalty, when he was arrested and convicted for the seventh time, he was given his choice: lifetime imprisonment without parole, or banishment to a new world.

He chose the banishment.

He rejected the first three worlds they chose. It then occurred to the authorities that he had no choice in the matter, but because he had made such a fuss they decided to send him to world with which they had never had any contact. It was a planet known to its inhabitants as Earth, and it would be very difficult for him to cause the kind of disturbances there that he had caused on Grafipo. Earth had no video. It had no computers. It had only discovered the principles of flight within the past dozen years. Still, his captors knew B'narr. The trick would be to put him down in an unpopulated (or at least underpopulated) area, where his capacity for mischief would be severely limited.

A thorough survey by a trio of computerized drones concluded that there were a number of vast, empty deserts on the planet. The problem, they realized, is that sooner or later he could find his way to civilization, and based on their knowledge of him, civilization didn't need the added problems he would bring.

They studied the surveys further, and finally hit upon a solution, not an ideal one but as close as they could come. They would deposit him on the slopes of a mountain after planting an identifying chip in his body. Then they would create an invisible barrier entirely around the base of the mountain, one that would recognize the chip but would permit every other living creature to pass.

It then became a matter of choosing the mountain. The most impressive was Everest, but the one that seemed farthest from any substantial center of population was Kilimanjaro, and they chose the latter for that reason.

It was not much later that a small ship entered the atmosphere and approached the snow-capped mountain.

"Remember," said one of the officers. "You can never leave the mountain."

"I trust you don't mind if I try," replied B'narr.

"Not at all," said the officer. "It won't hurt *me*."

The ship hovered above a grass-covered ridge about halfway up the mountain.

"This is where you leave us," said another officer, opening the hatch.

"If you had just learned to keep your mouth shut..." said the first officer.

"In twenty seconds I will have more freedom than you have ever known," said B'narr. "I would not trade places with you for anything."

"It's probably good that you feel that way," said the first office, "since you will live and die on this forsaken alien mountain."

B'narr walked to the hatch, and was soon being lowered to the surface. A moment later he was standing on his new world, the hatch closed, and the ship began racing for the stratosphere.

B'narr put his hands on his hips and took his first long look at the mountain where he would live and die. He knew that some of the fruits and animals would be edible; they wouldn't have spent millions flying him here just to let him die of systemic poisoning or starvation in the first few weeks. He looked down and saw the footprints of an elephant. He had no idea what the beast looked like, but given its size he hoped that it wasn't a carnivore.

Avians sang in the trees. He studied them until he was convinced that they presented no threat. He could see a village perhaps a mile away, but he decided not to try to make contact until he knew more about the inhabitants. He couldn't imagine that his captors had chosen a mechanized or sophisticated world for him – and there was no sense showing himself to a people who probably didn't know any other sentient species existed, at least until he studied them further and felt confident of a non-violent reception.

Suddenly he heard a roar. It wasn't close, but it was loud enough to convince him that his first order of business was to find a sanctuary where he could sleep in safety.

He began walking. As he did so he passed a number of caves, but he couldn't be sure that they weren't home to whatever had roared. He considered climbing a tree and sleeping on a broad branch, but he couldn't be sure he wouldn't fall off, and besides there was every possibility that at least one carnivore was arboreal.

He continued exploring his surroundings. After two more hours it began getting darker, and he realized that he didn't know the planet's rotation speed, and hence the length of its days and nights. He looked toward the top of the mountain. The dense vegetation thinned out the higher he went, and seemed to vanish entirely at the edge of the glacier.

It was an easy decision. Until he knew the mountain and its residents – sentient and otherwise – better, he'd spend his time up near the ice cap, where there was less vegetation, because less vegetation meant less herbivores and less herbivores means less meat-eaters. They might even avoid the glacier entirely.

He trudged up the mountain, alert to every sound and movement, and made it to his destination without seeing a single animal. He found the edge of the glacier cold, but not unbearably so, and he began looking for shelter. He found a cave, made sure that it bore no trace of any other resident, and entered it. He was aware that the air was much thinner up here, but his body adjusted to it and he paid it no further notice.

He awoke from his first night on his new world, stepped out into the sunlight, and walked down to the tree line. His first task was to find some nourishment, and he tried some nuts from one of the trees. They didn't have much taste, but they didn't do him any harm, and he began sampling fruits, grasses, barks, and other nuts, making mental notes about which tasted better. When he had satisfied his appetite, he decided self-defense was the next order of business. He found some flat stones just below the edge of the glacier, appropriated the two sharpest of them, tore a straight branch off a tree, and spent the next few hours working on it with the stones until he had a formidable spear. One of the stones was almost the right shape to double as a dagger, and he created a necklace of woven grasses to hold it.

He saw some small antelope and a variety of rodents, all of them moving very cautiously, which implied to him that predators *did* reach this altitude. Just at twilight he impaled a spring hare with his spear, and took it back to his cave with him, where he ate the meaty parts and buried the rest beneath the snow so that it wouldn't attract any predators.

That was his routine for the next month. Each day he went a little farther afield, either at the same altitude or a bit lower. By the end of the month he had seen elephant, rhino, buffalo, and leopards, plus smaller game, but he still hadn't seen any member of the sentient species. He decided that was his next step.

There was a village about two miles away from his cave, mostly to the south and also a few thousand feet lower in altitude. Were it not for their nightly fires he would not have known for sure it was still populated, for they made almost no noise and never climbed higher up the mountain. He decided that twilight was the best time to approach it. It would be too hard for him to hide in the daylight, and he wouldn't be able to observe them once the fires went out at night.

So he very carefully made his way to the village, a series of some thirty huts, and hid behind a large tree while the women prepared their food over the open fires. He'd been eating his food raw since he'd arrived, and while he hadn't suffered any ill effects, he made a mental note to try cooking it as these beings did to see if it made it any tastier.

One of the men came over and said something to a woman. She replied, he frowned and spoke again, she yelled at him, and he shrugged and walked away. B'narr wished this society had language and educator disks that he could tie into, so that he could learn their speech and their customs in a day or two while he slept. But clearly they didn't, and he was going to have to do it the hard way. If he was going to share the mountain with them, it was counter-productive not to be able to communicate with them…and if their reaction was hostile, he would at least be able to explain that he, too, was a sentient being.

It wasn't easy. He learned only twenty-seven words in the first two weeks. But he hid near the huts every night, and before too many months had passed he was able to understand almost half the exchanges. By the time he'd been observing and listening for a year, he considered himself reasonably fluent, though his elongated foreface could not pronounce the words quite the way the men and women did.

On the night he decided he was ready to show himself, he elected to do it before the sun had set. He didn't want anyone mistaking him for a large cat in the dark, especially since he had seen a handful of black leopards over the past few months.

He waited until most of the village was gathered around their fires, eating their evening meal. Then he raised his voice as much as he could without it turning into a yell.

"I bid you greetings," he said in Swahili. "I am a stranger, alone and helpless. I mean you no harm."

"Where are you?" demanded one of the men, looking around.

"I will show myself in a moment," said B'narr. "But first I must warn you that I do not look like you. Please do not be frightened. I wish only to be your friend."

"Show yourself," said another man, "and we shall decide."

B'narr leaned his spear up against the tree behind which he had been hiding, then removed his grass necklace and dagger as well, in the hope that appearing unarmed would convince them he was no threat. Then he walked to the edge of the village.

Three of the women screamed, and every man, without exception, grabbed a spear or a bow and arrow and faced him. A little girl, totally naked, perhaps two years old, approached him fearlessly, and before anyone could stop her or call to her, she ran right up to him and wrapped her arms around his leg. He reached down and gently stroked her hair.

"Who are you?" demanded the man who seemed to be their leader. "And *what* are you?"

He knew from a year of observing and listening to them that they were unaware of any other planets in *this* star system, let alone in any other, and they would never be able to comprehend the truth. So instead he said, "I was born of normal parents, just like you. But because I am so different they abandoned me. I have been living up there" – he pointed to the glacier – "ever since. But food has become scarce, and I decided it was time to live with men again – if you will have me."

"We will consider your request," said the leader.

"I will wait," said B'narr.

"Come back tomorrow. We will have an answer then."

He gently extricated himself from the little girl's grasp, turned, and began walking back to where he had left his weapons. The girl began crying, ran after him, and once again wrapped her arms around his leg. He bent over and reached down for her. She released her grasp when she felt his hands on her, and he carried her to the nearest woman, who took her from him.

That may have been beneficial, he thought as he walked away. *At least they know children are not afraid of me, and that I have no interest in harming or stealing them.*

He retrieved his weapons, and made his way up the mountain to his cave. He was up at sunrise, and this time he did not wait until twilight to approach the village but walked openly into it at noon.

The leader emerged from his hut and approached him.

"My name is Goru," he said. "This is my village. If you do no harm, you will be welcome here."

"Thank you," said B'narr.

"Bira thinks you are a devil, and he will be watching you closely."

"Who is Bira?"

"Our *mundumugu.*"

"*Mundumugu?*" repeated B'narr.

"He who makes the laws," explained Goru.

A wizened old man approached them. "I can speak for myself," he said.

"You are Bira?" asked B'narr.

"I am Bira, creature," he answered. "And I know you for what you are."

"I wish only to befriend your people and be of service to them," B'narr assured him.

"If that is true, we will hide you when the Germans come," said Goru. "Or if we have ample warning, you will retreat to where you live now until they have gone."

"What are Germans?" asked B'narr.

"Europeans."

"And what are Europeans?"

"Unlike you, they are *men,*" interjected Bira.

"They are white men who have superior weapons," continue Goru. "They came to the land many years ago, when I was still a child, and declared that it was theirs and not ours."

"And they have driven all your people to this mountain?"

Goru shook his head. "No. My tribe has always lived on Kilimanjaro. But many tribes live on Serengeti and near Ngorongoro and Olduvai, and the Germans rule us all."

"How many Germans are there?"

Goru shrugged. "Who can know? They come from a land that is far away."

"So only some of them live here?" persisted B'narr.

"That is correct."

"How many?"

Another shrug. "I don't know. A hundred. A thousand. A million. *Enough.*"

"Are any on the mountain right now?"

"I do not think so," said Goru. "But Kilimanjaro is a big mountain."

"Perhaps we should talk about these Germans," said B'narr.

"That is what we have been doing," said Goru, confused.

"I mean everyone who lives on Kilimanjaro."

"Why?"

"Because it is *our* mountain, not the Germans'," answered B'narr. "We must find a way to let the Germans know that."

"We cannot fight them," said Goru.

B'narr smiled a very alien smile. "There are ways," he said. "We will discuss it tomorrow."

"My magic cannot defeat them," said Bira. "If yours can, it is more proof that you are a devil."

"I am not a devil," answered B'narr. "And there is something else I am not: a *mundumugu.* You are the only one in this village. I do not want your job."

"You do not think it is worthy of you?" spat Bira.

"I am just a stranger who wishes to help." B'narr spent an hour in the village, learning the people's names, learning who lived in which hut, learning where the other villages on this side of the mountain were and which tribes lived in them, and then he went back to his cave with a sense of deep satisfaction.

They *needed* him.

Far from being banished here, he now knew that he'd been put here for a purpose. He suddenly felt complete again.

The next morning he returned to the village. He had hoped to find some fifty village leaders gathered there. Instead there were only eighteen, plus Goru and Bira, but he wasn't discouraged. One had to start somewhere.

"I am pleased to meet you all," he said by way of greeting. "I will learn each of your names before the meeting is over."

"What *are* you?" the tallest of the leaders,

"I thought Goru had explained it to you," said B'narr.

"Bira is right," replied the man. "You were never born of human parents."

"I know it is difficult to believe…" began B'narr.

"It is *impossible* to believe. What tribe do you belong to?"

"Until yesterday I lived by myself since I was a child," answered B'narr, "so it was a tribe of one. But now I declare myself a member of the tribe of men that live on the slopes of Kilimanjaro."

"I do not like this person, Goru," said the tall man. "He will not answer my questions."

"I told you he wouldn't," said Bira emphatically.

"That is not so," said B'narr. "I have answered your questions. You just do not like my answers, which is not the same thing." He looked at the assembled leaders. "But when we talk about the Germans, I think you will like my answers then."

"How do we know you are not in league with them?" asked another leader.

"How could I be?" replied B'narr. "I have spent my whole life higher on the mountain than this village. Have the Germans ever come this high?"

"No," admitted the man. "But if you have never seen a German, why are you opposed to them?"

"Because everyone who lives on the mountain is my brother, and they have no right to give my brothers orders."

"You are not *my* brother!" snapper Bira.

"Bira fears that I wish to replace him as *mundumugu*," said B'narr. "I do not. He is a small, jealous man, but his jealousy is misplaced. I want only to show you how to rid yourselves of the Germans."

There was a momentary silence. Then the tall leader said, "You ,may speak. We will listen to you."

"That is all I ask," said B'narr. "This will take time. Why don't you all sit down?"

They seemed surprised by the request, but they did as he asked, except for Bira, who remained standing.

"Let us begin," he said, "by examining how best to protest any demands the Germans make upon you. Do they conscript you for their army?"

"No."

"Do they tax you?"

"One pig per hut," was the answer.

"Every year?"

"Whenever they come."

"Since you cannot match weaponry with them, you must be more clever," said B'narr. "And you must work in unison. Each village must designate two or three boys as runners."

"Runners?" asked another leader.

"Bear with me. We never want the Germans to surprise us with a visit, so we will post seven or eight boys along the approach trails, and whenever they see the Germans coming they will race back to the mountain and tell the lowest villages. Runners from those villages will each go to a designated village and pass the word, so that everyone will know, and most will know before the Germans reach the mountain." B'narr looked at his audience, which was suddenly paying rapt attention. "Now, beginning tomorrow, we will build an enclosure in the thickest part of the highest forest on the mountain. And whenever we know that the Germans are approaching, the children from each hut will drive the pigs up to the enclosure."

"They will not all go," said a leader.

"Yes they will," said B'narr, "because the day the pen is finished, your children, under your supervision, will drive the pigs up to it once a week, until it becomes routine to them. Then, when the Germans enter the villages, you will explain that a disease has wiped out all your pigs." Suddenly he smiled. "You can even ask them to replace the pigs, since they are in charge of the country."

Goru chuckled at that.

"They will just find something else they want," said the tall leader.

"Then we will adapt our strategy to accommodate whatever it is they want," said B'narr. "Not only that, but we will use our runners to pass the word of our accomplishments to all the villages that are near the mountain, and encourage them to pass the strategy along until the whole country knows of it."

"It will be much harder to hide pigs on flat ground," said another leader.

"We will help them think of ways to hide them. Do not forget: yesterday you would have said you could not hide your villages' pigs so that the Germans could not find them."

"Sooner or later they will find then, or they will ask for something else," said a leader. "Our women, perhaps."

"This is just the first step," said B'narr. "You say they have superior weapons?"

"Yes."

"Do they claim *all* of Africa?"

"What is Africa?" asked one of the leaders.

"Do they claim all the land there is?" said B'narr, re-wording the question.

"No. Only Tanganyka."

"But why, if they have the best weapons?"

"The British have similar weapons."

B'narr smiled. "And where are the British?"

"I do not know where they come from," said the leader, "but they rule Kenya."

"Where is Kenya?"

The leader pointed to the north. "There."

"How far is it?"

"A day's march, maybe a little less."

"There is your answer," said B'narr.

He was met with confused frowns.

"The Germans didn't invent their powerful weaponry to conquer *you*. So they must have created it to match some other tribe's weaponry, and you have told me that tribe is the British. After the first step, which is hiding the pigs, the Germans will demand something else. Then you will send representatives to the British a day's march away and complain about your treatment at the Germans' hands and tell them that you would much rather be ruled by them. And at the same time, you will have Kenyan tribes on the other side of the border complain to the Germans that they cannot stand British rule."

Suddenly there were smiles among his audience.

"You will volunteer to help each side as camp attendants. You will cook and wash their clothes and do whatever menial tasks they give you. And every time a soldier from either side dies in battle, you will appropriate his weapon and ammunition. When the military you are serving is small enough, you will poison their food. If it is larger, you will find ways, through children who are always above suspicion, to let the other side know where it is. And when the two sides have decimated each other, and one is totally destroyed or at least so badly beaten that it gives up all claim to any territory, you will have enough weaponry and enough experience to annihilate the winning side." He paused. "It will not happen overnight, and it will not be easy. But if you are determined enough, it *can* happen."

"You look like a monster," said the tallest leader. "But you think like a *laibon* or a *mundumugu*." He stared coldly at Bira. "Why did our own *mundumugu* never think of these things."

Bira made no answer, but simply glared hatefully at B'narr.

"I have a question," said Goru.

"Yes?" said B'narr.

"What will *you* want for all this?" said Goru. "Do you wish to be acknowledged the *jumbe kwa kijumbe*?"

"The chief of chiefs?" repeated B'narr. He shook his head. "No, I have no desire to rule anyone. I am interested only in seeing justice done."

"Truly?"

"Truly."

"You make it hard to think of you as a man," said Goru.

The other leaders laughed at that, all except Bira.

"We will meet again every day until we have every detail planned," said B'narr. "We must know exactly where to build the enclosure. We must make certain there are no impassable hazards for the pigs that are lower down the mountain. We must know which boys we are going to trust to be our runners. We must map out their routes not only on the mountain but on the plains beyond the mountain. We must be prepared for every eventuality. I have given you a lot to think about. I suggest you go back to your villages and consider what I have said, and we will meet here at the same hour tomorrow."

The men left, and B'narr returned to the glacier. He considered building a hut – he'd seen them constructed in a matter of hours – and joining the village, but decided his voice would carry more authority if he was not a member of any particular village.

They met the next day, and the day after that, and after that. They built the enclosure in such a spot that it could not be seen from more than a few hundred feet away, and then they practiced running the pigs up to it. The boys who had been chosen to be the runners were drilled over and over again.

And then came the day they had been waiting for. A squad of German soldiers visited the mountain and demanded their porcine tax. Village after village explained that a disease had wiped out all the pigs.

The Germans entered every hut, certain that the villagers were hiding pigs

— and finally one of the Germans called the others over to a spot just beyond the village.

"Look!" he said, pointing at a pile of dung. "That is *fresh*! These people are lying to us!"

From his vantage point on the glacier B'narr saw that the Germans had reached the mountain. That didn't surprise him. The whole plan depended on their coming sooner or later. But then he heard the rifle shots. *That* surprised him. There was a shot every ten minutes, from mid-morning to late afternoon.

He decided to make sure the Germans were gone before he appeared, so he remained where he was until sunrise, when he made his way down to the Goru's village. To his surprise he found all the leaders waiting for him.

"How did it go?" he asked.

"While you hid on your glacier, the Germans killed one child from every village!" snarled Goru, his face reflecting his rage and hatred.

"We listened to you instead of to Bira," said the tall leader. "We will never make that mistake again."

"What happened?" demanded B'narr.

"What happened is our fault for listening to a creature that pretends to be a man. Instead, let me tell you what *will* happen. You will return to the snow and ice, and you will live out your life there. If any of us ever sees you below the snow after today, we will kill you, slowly and painfully."

"But how did the Germans find out?" insisted B'narr. "Didn't you move all the pigs?"

"I will count to fifty," said the tall leader. "If you are still here when I am finished, I will kill you myself."

B'narr looked from one face to another, and could find nothing but hatred and fury. He turned and began running up to the ice cap. There were no sounds of pursuit, and he slowed to a fast walk after a few minutes.

As he reached the tree line, he found Bira waiting for him.

"I *told* them you were a devil," he said. "In the end my magic was stronger than yours."

"Magic had nothing to do with it," said B'narr wearily.

"We will call it magic when I speak to my people," answered Bira. A nasty smile crossed his face. "Whether it was magic or something else that moved the pig's dung to where the Germans could not help but find it, the result was the same."

"But why?" asked B'narr, truly puzzled.

"Because I am the *mundumugu*, and this mountain and this tribe do not need another."

B'narr was about to answer when armed warriors approached at a run, and he had to retreat to the glacier.

The next morning he was beginning to move past the tree line to go hunting for his breakfast when he found himself facing three young men armed with spears.

"Go back, creature!" yelled one of them. "You are not allowed here!"

He retreated to the glacier, and walked totally around it over the next five days. Whenever he thought he had gone far enough and tried to go down past the tree line he was confronted by armed warriors.

He didn't give up. He circled the entire glacier regularly, but every time he tried to climb down off it he found his path barred.

Weak from hunger and exhaustion, he finally returned to his cave. *This cannot be my fault*, he thought. *I have organized far more difficult and complicated protests. They messed it up. But how?*

He lay there for three days. He knew he was dying, and he found he didn't mind that at all. If he was forbidden from doing what he was born to do, then life was meaningless anyway. But before he expired, he *had* to find out what had gone wrong.

He got shakily to his feet, and was overwhelmed by dizziness and nausea. He leaned against a cave wall for a moment, then another, and finally he emerged onto the glacier. He walked laboriously for ten minutes, having difficulty balancing on the ice. The sun seemed exceptionally bright, and his eyes began tearing. He reached a hand up to wipe them off – and as he did so he lost his balance and fell heavily to the ice.

He tried to get up and found that he couldn't. He could feel his life ebbing away. Breathing became more difficult. He tried to focus his eyes, but everything remained blurry.

It shouldn't have come to this, he thought bitterly. *It was a perfect plan. Whatever happened, I wasn't the one who failed. You should have been cheering me and singing my praises by now.*

He knew he would be dead in another few seconds, and one final thought crossed his mind:

I hope the Germans kill you all.

2038 A.D.

"I'm starting to think that Hemingway never got up this high," said Ray Glover. "After all, he was an out-of-shape boozer. I'm in great shape and I still can't catch my breath."

"He was a fiction writer," said Jim Donahue. "So it's possible he made it up. After all, in *The Green Hills of Africa*, which is still being sold as non-fiction, he seems to run into someone who wants to discuss literature every time he's hiding in a blind waiting for some animal to come by, and no one ever called him on that."

"If you go up and down the Coast, you can still find half a dozen hotels that brag that 'Hemingway Slept Here'," said Gorman. "According to the stories that have been passed down, he mostly drank there and slept where he fell or passed out."

"Still, wouldn't it be something if we *could* find the leopard?" I said.

"We've already found something a thousand times more important," replied Donahue. "Maybe ten professors of literature give a damn whether the leopard was real or not, but if *this*" – he indicated the frozen body – "is what we all think it is, *everyone* will care."

"Could it have been a snow leopard?" asked Glover. "I remember seeing one in a zoo once. That wouldn't be so hard to believe, would it?"

"You find a snow leopard up here and you got a real story," said Gorman. "They only live in Asia."

Glover turned to me. "Is that right, Professor?"

"Doctor," I said. "Or just Tony. And yes, it's right. There are no snow leopards in Africa."

"Papa would never have bothered writing the story if there were," added Gorman.

"I wonder," said Donahue. "Could he have seen this fellow from a distance and *thought* it was a leopard?"

"Always assuming that it's been on the mountain that long, if Papa was close enough to know it was a body why didn't he walk the last couple of hundred feet and see what it was?" asked Gorman.

"Too drunk?" suggested Donahue.

"If he was that drunk, he wouldn't have spotted it or remembered it," said Gorman.

I noticed that Bonnie wasn't paying any attention to the conversation (not that it was worth listening to), but instead was staring intently at the body.

They're all wrong, she thought. The important thing isn't what he was doing atop Kilimanjaro, but what he was doing on Earth at all. I don't see any weapons, or any pouch or holster that might hold a weapon. Surely he didn't come here just to see the top of a mountain – and if he did, then why not Fuji or Everest or even Pike's Peak? Why this mountain? What secret was he trying to unearth? And no one else has remarked on the way his right hand seems to be reaching out. For what, I wonder? What could draw an unarmed alien to this place?

Bonnie Herrington, despite her gender, was the fifth blind man.

WHAT THE CAMERAWOMAN SAW

His name was Quachama, and he had devoted his life to finding God. Not the way televangelists and born-again Christians do. No, they were no closer to God than the man on the street. In fact, if they misinterpreted His signs and signals and spread them to the masses, they were actually further.

There was no mention ever made of God on his home planet. His race believed in self-sufficiency and hard work, they refused favors and had no use for sympathy or forgiveness, and somehow the notion of a Supreme Deity never took hold.

It was when he was studying other worlds' sentient races in school that Quachama first encountered the notion of God, and it fascinated him. If there *was* a God, why had He created the Universe, only to fill it with such suffering, so many hardships? Was it His purpose that each species would triumph over these obstacles? If it was, why did so many fail? And if it wasn't, why had He put them there in the first place? Why had He allowed some races to split the atom, cure disease, and develop space flight, while other races remained planetbound, sick, and in primitive conditions?

The most obvious question to ask the believers was: if He hasn't truly manifested Himself, if your brethren still suffer and die, then why do you still believe in Him? But Quachama had progressed beyond that question. He found that he did indeed believe in God, or some manifestation of Him, and he wanted to confront God and ask why He allowed anyone to suffer, or to fail at anything, or to hunger, or to die.

And he made it his life's work to seek God out, confront Him face-to-face, and demand an answer.

The first world he visited was Bellarnus, in the heart of the Nemacton Cluster. It was a water world, covered by an ocean, dotted with islands. The dominant race was a species of intelligent, mammalian seagoing creatures, not totally unlike dolphins, and their God was said to occupy an undersea castle two miles below the north magnetic pole. Quachama positioned his boat over the castle, donned his underwater gear, jumped into the ocean, and began swimming toward the castle. It took him four hours of careful descent, and when he reached the place where the castle was supposed to be, he found nothing but sand ad rocks. It took him three times as long to reach the surface, to avoid the possibility of depth sickness, and when he was back in his boat he related his experience to a member of the dolphin-like race who was swimming alongside.

"Ah!" was the answer. "God did not wish you to find Him. He can move his castle around the world at will."

"But *why* didn't He want me to find Him?" asked Quachama.

"Only God can answer that," said the dolphin. "Remain here. I am sure once God decides you mean Him no harm He will return."

"If He is God, then by definition I cannot harm Him," replied Quachama.

"Then perhaps He had some other reason for moving His castle."

"Have you personally seen this castle?" asked Quachama.

"I am not religious. I have never had a reason to look for it."

"Do you know *anyone* who has seen it?"

"Probably. It is not something we talk about in polite company. After all, He is God."

His mind made up, Quachama began climbing out of his diving gear. "Thank you for your trouble," he said.

"You are not going to wait for God?" asked the dolphin.

"No."

"That's all right. He will know how to find you."

"We shall see," said Quachama.

That was the first of twenty-seven worlds he visited, searching for God. He looked in the jungles of Selamun, the endless desert of Tilanbo, the underground caverns of Jebb, and always he concluded that God did not dwell on that particular world.

His belief in God remained unshaken, but he became a lot more cynical about the claims made by God's self-appointed spokesmen and worshippers. Still, he had no alternative but to continue his quest. He prayed every morning and every night, but God never acknowledged receiving the prayers, never once manifested Himself to Quachama, which simply made it more important than ever that the two of them should meet face-to-face, for that was the only way Quachama could be sure that God actually heard him.

He almost died in the asteroid belt between the sixth and seventh planets of the Amatiro system. He thought he got a glimpse of God on Tzintrep, but he got lost in the maze of corridors and tunnels beneath the Great Temple, and by the time he got his bearings and made his way back to the Throne Room of the Almighty, the place was deserted, and it stayed deserted for the twelve days that he remained there.

He realized that he was getting older, that he did not have an infinite amount of time in which to hunt for God on an infinite number of worlds. He determined that he would be more selective in his choice of venues, he would study each world more thoroughly, and he would visit the world only when he felt there was a reasonable chance that he had come at last to God's world.

For those reasons, Graetep, Promandios, Chovnost, and Litantia seemed very promising, but alas, none of the four delivered on their promises. He was getting desperate now, running low on money, low on energy, low on years remaining to him.

And then he discovered Earth.

He had long known about it, a gritty little world that was always going to war with itself, but remained isolated from the rest of the galaxy because its technology was in its infancy, a lovely green and gold world with an acceptable gravity and atmosphere.

But the fascinating thing was that while every other world had but a single religion, or none at all, Earth had a plethora of religions, and many of them possessed first-hand accounts of meetings with God (and a major one had eyewitness accounts of God's death by crucifixion). That was the key: how could so many religions believe God dwelt there if there was absolutely no truth to it?

He spent a week pouring over the holy books of the various religions, and another studying the geography and culture of the planet. He knew he couldn't pass for a member of the dominant race of man, but he learned that he could mask his features with a hooded robe and possibly some gloves, and he would be accepted as a religious acolyte and move unchallenged through most of the holy places.

He captured some sound transmissions in the hope of learning the language, and was shocked to find there were hundreds of languages. His computer suggested that if he gained a rudimentary knowledge of English, French, Spanish, Arabic and Chinese, he could function in most venues. Fortunately languages came easily to him, and with the computer's help he picked them up during his six-week journey to Earth.

He had the locations listed by priority. He activated his ship's cloaking device, landed in Sinai, donned the hooded robe he had prepared, traveled on foot by night and hid by day, and finally reached Golgotha.

There was nothing to mark that this was the spot where so many people had seen their God, or His Earthly manifestation, but Quachama had done his research, and was able to pinpoint the spot on what was now known as Gordon's Calvary where the cross had been planted. It was the middle of the night when he approached it, the only living being within fifty yards. He made sure no one was around to over-hear, and then he spoke:

"God, are You here?"

There was no answer, and he realized he had spoken in his native tongue. He repeated the query in English and Arabic. Still no answer. He wondered if he was supposed to address God only in Aramaic, the ancient language that was used during the crucifixion, but decided that if that was the case, everyone would still be speaking it.

He was disappointed, but not discouraged, and two days later he stood on slopes of Mount Olympus, addressing the Deity as both God and Zeus. Both, if they existed, ignored him.

He next went to Rome. There seemed to be no consensus as to where Jupiter lived, so he went from ruin to ruin, ad-dressing Him from the ruins of buildings that existed before Jupiter fell out of favor, to be replaced by Jesus in the hearts of his people.

Two weeks and eleven more false starts brought him to Africa, the last continent on which he might find God. When he saw the size of the Egyptian ruins he had a feeling that he was getting close, that surely the temples at Karnak and Edfu and Kom Ombo had been built for God's convenience. He went to each, imploring Ra, the Sun God, to speak to him. Ra remained silent, but rather than move on, Quachama also tried to converse with Anubis, Horus and Osiris, although with no better results.

He could feel his body breaking down, and knew that this would be his last planet, his last chance to put forward those questions he had been waiting all of his adult life to ask. He tried his luck at Abu Simbel, got no response, and headed south.

There were many variations of Islam, but he'd been to Mecca and other holy sites, and since he'd received no heav-enly response there and time was becoming a consideration, he chose not to further pursue the God of Mohammed in

Africa. But the computer uncovered some other religions, each with their own God, or their own interpretation of the same God, and he decided that they were different enough from those he had tried that they were worth his few remaining attempts.

The first was the mountain Kirinyaga, known to most settlers and tourists as Mount Kenya. But he wasn't interested in the tourists and settlers, most of whom worshiped the God of the Christians and the Jews, a God Who had already repulsed his attempts to communicate. No, Kirinyaga was the holy mountain of the Kikuyu people, and the reason it was holy was because their God, Ngai, lived atop it.

He found a flat, empty strip of ground at eleven thousand feet, set his ship down, and cloaked it. A bongo and her foal watched him curiously as he climbed down from the hatch. He looked up the mountain and saw the ice-covered peak about six thousand feet above him. It would not be a straight or an easy climb, especially in the dark – he was still making sure that nobody saw him, as this world wouldn't be ready for interstellar contact for a very long time – but he was resigned to it. Earlier in his travels, he would have made it in a single night, or at most two. But that was thirty-five years ago. This time it would take the better part of six days, climbing by night, hiding by day. At fourteen thousand feet the vegetation thinned out and would soon cease, but he was so tired, so short of breath, that he actually slowed his pace.

He reached the summit on the eighth day, and looked around for signs that God lived atop the mountain.

"Ngai, are you here?" he asked. "I must speak with you, and I haven't got much time left."

But if Ngai was there, He chose not to answer.

Quachama remained near the summit for another day, partially to regain some of his strength, partially to give Ngai a chance to reconsider if He was there but in hiding.

Finally he began his descent. When he reached the ship he collapsed and slept for two days and two nights. When he awoke, he knew that his next attempt would be his last, and that he must choose his venue very carefully.

The computer thought the God of the Zulus was his best remaining chance, but before he laid in a course for Natal, he saw that there was a similar religion to the Kikuyu, from a tribe that had gone to war with the Kikuyu many times and never lost. They were the Maasai, and their God, named En-Kai, lived atop the greatest mountain on the continent, a mountain known as Kilimanjaro.

He studied further, but his mind was racing ahead of the computer. Ngai and En-kai. Kirinyaga and Kilimanjaro. The more he thought about it, the more he thought that, at least in terms of religion, the Kikuyu were a pale imitation of the Maasai. He asked the computer to give him a breakdown of the Kikuyu's religious beliefs. Twenty-one percent believed in the traditional religion; seventy-nine percent had converted to some form of Christianity. He asked for the same breakdown of the Maasai. Ninety-three percent believe in En-kai, seven percent were Christians.

Now he knew why he had received no response atop Kirinyaga. Just as the Maasai had conquered the Kikuyu, En-kai had conquered the false god Ngai, who had even tried to steal His name. He would go to Kilimanjaro, and after a lifetime of searching, he would finally find God and get his answers.

He landed his ship on one of the lower slopes and activated the cloaking mechanism, then began climbing. An elephant charged him as he crossed a clearing, and he was barely able to clamber up a tree before it reached the spot he had been. It stood beneath the tree for four hours, but eventually it lost interest and wandered away, and he climbed down and began ascending the mountain again.

He saw a leopard depositing its kill in the fork of a tree, but it paid him no attention, and he continued walking. His energy was ebbing, he was in constant pain, and he no longer cared whether he was seen or not. He would climb night and day, stopping only when he was so exhausted or in such pain that he could not continue without resting, and as soon as he was able he would begin again.

He reached the tree line in three days and, taking one last look down the mountain, he strode onto the glacier.

At one point he could go no farther without resting, and he sat down, hunched over, and looked down the mountain, then out across the savanna. *This must be God's home*, he thought. *Who else could create such an awesome mountain, or such a magnificent vista? And all of His creatures share Kilimanjaro with men. I have finally reached the place I was searching for all these years.*

He decided it was time to continue his climb, and he prepared to get up – and found that he couldn't. He tried again, and his legs simply wouldn't work.

I am dying, he thought. *It seems fitting, somehow, that I should die on God's mountain, now that I have finally found it.*

And as his vision became blurry, he thought he saw an incredible brightness approaching him.

I have been waiting for you, said the brightness silently, the words echoing inside his head. *Now we shall finally have our talk.*

He still couldn't rise, but he reached out a hand toward En-kai.

2038 A.D.

Jim Donahue had finished taking his pictures, and put his camera back in its case. Not so Bonnie Herrington. She and Ray Glover were going around to each member of the party, interviewing them, asking not only for their reactions to what we'd found but their speculations as to what it might be.

I could tell that Charles Njobo was torn about what to say. He *wanted* to claim that it was an extraterrestrial visitor, but he was painfully aware that, as he kept reminding us, he represented the Tanzanian government, and he didn't want to make a statement that could embarrass the government if it turned out to be wrong.

While they were doing their interviews, I walked over to the body again, and tried to figure out what the hell it was doing above the tree line on the tallest mountain on the continent.

An interstellar sportsman, climbing Kilimanjaro for the challenge of it? But he had no climbing gear, at least none that I could see, and if he could make it all the way to this mountain from some other star system, he could have gone a few thousand miles farther to the Himalayas. Everest had to be two miles higher.

A hunter, perhaps? If he'd arrived more than seventy-five years ago, Tanzania was so thick with game that it must have seemed like it would go on forever. The wildebeest herds numbered in the millions, the zebras were almost as numerous, and the Big Five – elephant, rhino, lion, buffalo, and leopard – were abundant on both the ground and the mountain.

But he had no weapons, there was no trace of a camp, and if he'd stockpiled any trophies they'd been appropriated by some resident of the mountain or perhaps a climber – but if they'd found his trophies, they'd almost certainly have found him as well.

All my training, all my experience, told me that he wasn't a freak born of Earth. No human, no ape, nothing of this world ever gave birth to the being that lay before me. He must have come from a relatively similar world. If the gravity were much heavier he'd have thicker limbs and would probably walk on all fours; any lighter and he'd be thinner and more elongated. It had to be an oxygen world; he couldn't have gone two steps, let alone up the mountain, if he couldn't breathe the air. I assumed he could metabolize some of the vegetation or meat animals, since there was no indication he'd come with a sufficient supply of his own food – though I wouldn't know for sure until we thawed him out and examined his teeth and the contents of his stomach. The ears weren't much bigger than ours; the eyes were closed, but also seemed about the same size as ours. The elongated foreface implied that scent was more important to him, but even that was just a guess until we began examining him in a lab.

I was suddenly aware that Bonnie and Ray were approaching me.

"Your turn, Professor," she said cheerfully.

"Call me Doctor," I said. "Or better still, Anthony or Tony."

"How about Doc?"

I shrugged. "That'll be fine."

Ray reached over and attached a tiny microphone to the collar of my coat.

"Don't worry about it," said Bonnie. "It won't show up in the video."

Why would I give a damn? I thought, but I merely smiled at her.

"Well, let's get right to it, Doc," she said. "What do you think of our discovery?"

"I think it could be very important," I said carefully. "Of course, we'll have to examine it under laboratory conditions before we can draw any firm conclusions."

"Jim Donahue keeps calling it a man from Mars," said Bonnie. "Would you care to comment on that?"

I smiled. "Jim has a fine imagination. It didn't come from Mars."

"Where *did* it come from?"

"I have no idea."

"Would you care to suggest what it's doing here?"

"Waiting to be discovered and evaluated," I said.

"Besides that," she said, a note of irritation creeping into her voice. "Why would this creature, whatever it is, climb the tallest mountain in Africa?"

Because it's there, I wanted to say. "I really don't know, Bonnie," I said aloud. "Scientists don't jump to conclusions."

She ended the interview in another minute, clearly disappointed, and wandered off to interview Njobo.

As for me, I looked down at the alien, and the phrase kept running through my mind again and again: *Because it's there.*

✦

I was the sixth blind man.

WHAT THE SCIENTIST SAW

His name was Mavorine, and he felt like the King of the Universe, standing atop the highest mountain on Neffertine VI, staring out across the craggy surface of the planet. This one would put him in the record books. No member of his race had ever climbed a mountain on a chlorine world before.

It had been a long, hard month. The mountain offered very little shelter from the fierce winds, and handholds and footholds were difficult to find on the final ascent. He stood at the summit, hands on hips, reporting everything he saw into the tiny recorder that was built into his helmet, activating the camera atop the helmet, turning his head slowly from side to side to capture the view.

He spent a day and a night at the mountaintop, then began the precarious descent. By the time he was halfway down he was already planning his next adventure, his next pursuit of the immortality afforded him by the record of his accomplishments. He wasn't limited to mountain climbing; that was simply his most recent passion. His first major triumph had come nine years earlier when he circumnavigated Balinoppe II's murky ocean, not in a vessel but on foot, on the ocean floor, emerging only eight times to replenish his oxygen supply.

He had been back from Balinoppe for only three days when he was off again, this time to far Perradorn, home to the galaxy's largest known carnivore species. They presented no serious problem to anyone armed with a modern weapon – an energy pulse rifle, or something similar – but no one had ever hunted one armed only with a poison-tipped spear . He spent four months in hospital recovering from his wounds…but the carnivore would spend an eternity stuffed and mounted in the Great Museum on his home world of Thandor IV.

After that had come the conquests of more mountains and oceans, more entries in the record books. He had mapped and captured holographs of worlds no one else had ever set foot on, and had become a hero to his people, idolized by most of them.

And while adults created entertainments about him, and children worshipped him, and grown males envied him, and females adored him, he spent a few days in his private dwelling. It had actually become unfamiliar to him, so infrequently did he spend more than a single night there. His computer kept going through its database, suggesting possibilities for his next adventure. Mavorine rejected them all.

"It is just another mountain," he would say. "Bigger than the last, but just a mountain."

Or: "I have walked across the floor of an ocean. I don't have to do it again."

After an hour had passed, he gave the computer a new order: "Just show me a series of worlds and their most dangerous or challenging features. Let us see if we can find one that is sufficiently interesting."

For the next two hours the computer showed him methane worlds, chlorine worlds, ammonia worlds, oxygen worlds, and airless worlds.

"Stop," he said at last. He sighed deeply. "I would not have believed it possible, but I have run out of challenges. These worlds are not without their interest and their challenges, but in truth it is just more of the same."

"Perhaps you should set yourself a different task," suggested the computer.

"What else is there?" he asked. "I have climbed, and swum, and mapped, and killed, and explored."

"The difference is in the matter of approach," answered the computer.

"Explain," said Mavorine.

"In every endeavor, it has been your goal to triumph, to succeed, to *accomplish*."

"What else is there?"

"Survival."

"I do not understand," said Mavorine.

"Ignore the record books," replied the computer. "Set yourself a task where merely surviving will be the ultimate triumph. Do not publicize it until you have survived and returned here to Thandor IV."

"Why not?"

"Because if you do, some other member of your race will doubtless try to emulate you, and he will surely die."

"Why does a machine care if a sentient being dies?"

"There is a chance that they will blame you, and if you are made to suffer for your competitor's shortcomings, then there is a strong possibility that I will be deactivated."

"Since when do you have a sense of self-preservation?"

"It is at least as strong as yours," said the computer reasonably. "I do not constantly put *my* existence at risk."

"This has been a most interesting discussion," said Mavorine. "I will consider it."

Which he did, and by the next morning he had become totally committed to the idea. Then it was just a matter of selecting the world that could offer him not the most awesome single challenge, but the greatest variety of challenges. Within a day he had narrowed his choice down to three worlds, and by the next evening he knew that his destination would be the planet known as Earth.

He would go there naked and unarmed, with no food supplies, no medical kit, absolutely nothing to help him. Then it became a matter of selecting the challenges.

He would climb the mountains known as Fujiyama, Everest, and Kilimanjaro. He would swim the width of the Indian Ocean. He would, with weapons he manufactured from the materials at hand, kill a tiger on one continent, a lion on another, and a jaguar on a third. He would swim down a pirhana-invested river. He would walk across the Sahara Desert. He had the computer order his itinerary, so he could go from one challenge to another with a minimum of time between them.

He told no one of his plans. When the itinerary was completed, he went to his ship, had the navigational computer lay in a course for Earth, and took off in the dead of night.

He realized that he couldn't possibly complete his quest if he were to move from challenge to challenge, alone and naked, not on an alien world that did not know of his world's existence. So he decided that he would activate the ship's cloaking device before it entered the stratosphere, and leave it on, flying unseen from one starting point to the next.

He began with Everest. He'd climbed taller, more formidable mountains elsewhere in the galaxy, while this was merely his first step. While he was in Asia, he crafted a bow and arrow and had very little difficulty killing a tiger in India.

He returned to his ship, flew to an uninhabited shore of the Indian Ocean, instructed it to land south of Mombasa in the Shimba Hills – he pinpointed the exact location since he wouldn't be able to see it – and then, as it took off, he plunged into the water. He spent most of his time in the midst of a pod of whales, which seemed not to mind his presence, and served to shield him from the interest of the sharks that patrolled the waters searching for prey. He learned that his system could tolerate raw fish, and he lived on them for the twenty-three days it took him to reach the African shore. He found himself halfway between Malindi and Mombasa, and he spent another day swimming south to where he could rejoin his ship.

He decided that he could accomplish his next two tasks at the same location. There would be lions on the lower slopes of Kilimanjaro. He would kill one, and then proceed to climb the mountain. He ordered the ship to take off and fly south and west until the snow-capped peak came into view. He landed at the foot of the mountain, waited until dark, and then emerged.

He carried the bow and arrows he had used to kill the tiger, and wondered if that was fair. Not that there were any rules that weren't of his own making, but he had a feeling that he should craft a fresh set of weapons to kill on a new continent. He ascended two thousand feet while he considered his moral dilemma, and decided that as long as he was still considering it, he should indeed create fresh weapons. It took him the next two nights – he remained in hiding in the thick bush during the day – but then he was ready to proceed.

His problem was that lions had no natural predators. They slept during the day, almost always in the open, but he could not chance being seen by the sentient residents of the mountain. And at night, along with the very poor visibility even when the moon was out, they were in hiding, preparing to attack unsuspecting prey.

He finally decided that if *he* were hunting prey on the forested and uneven surface of the mountain, he would hide near a waterhole and wait for his victim, so he chose a small one that seemed to attract a fair amount of game, took up his position behind a Wait-a-bit thorn tree, and settled down to wait for his prey as they hunted *their* prey.

An hour later a lone bushbuck cautiously approached the waterhole. Clearly it was nervous, and Mavorine decided that this was very unusual behavior, that usually the herbivores slaked their thirst in the light so they could see the approach of predators, but that this particular animal was simply too thirsty to wait for sunrise.

The bushbuck tested the air, sniffing furiously, and finally walked the last few feet to the waterhole and lowered its head to drink. It remained motionless, muzzle in the water, for almost half a minute. Then there was a horrendous, ear-shattering roar, and before the bushbuck could to more than lift its head to see where the enemy was, a lioness had burst from cover and gotten her fearsome jaws around its neck, cutting off its air supply. The bushbuck's struggles became more and more feeble, until finally it expired.

Mavorine was content to let her settle down and begin feeding so that she would present a stationery target, but instead she began dragging her kill off into the bush. He instantly stood up, put an arrow into his bow, and let fly. The lioness leaped high into the air, roaring furiously, and when she landed she began biting at the arrow in her side. He shot two more arrows into her, and a moment later she was as dead as her prey.

He suddenly became aware of the fact that he was bleeding, and realized that he'd managed to puncture his side and shoulder on the thorns as he stood up. He had no medication, of course, so he walked over to the waterhole, rinsed the blood off so that he wouldn't attract any lions or leopards, and slapped a little mud over the wounds. Then, because he had not had anything to drink all day, he knelt down and took a long drink from the waterhole.

He pulled his arrows out of the lioness. Not that he planned on using them again, even in self-defense; he had brand new arrows for that if it became necessary. But he was certain the sentient residents of the mountain had their own markings identifying their arrows, and he didn't want them looking for a stranger whose arrows could not be identified.

He considered going back to the ship, but decided there was no reason for it. After all, he was here not only to slay the lion but the climb the mountain.

He took one last look at the lioness and the bushbuck. He wished he had a knife so that he could cut off a piece of the bushbuck's haunch to eat. He considered the problem, then walked over, knelt down, and pulled at the small holes the lion's teeth had made while it was suffocating its prey. Some of the skin began parting, and he managed to rip off a piece of flesh. He stood up and looked down at the bushbuck. Yes, an observer would probably think the lioness had taken a bite of the bushbuck before she herself was killed.

He began chewing on the flesh as he ascended the mountain, keeping far from the villages. When the sun rose he was at an elevation of six thousand feet, and more than two miles from the nearest village. He saw no reason to stop, so he kept climbing.

He lay down beneath a thick bush at midday, thinking he'd get up at midnight and continue his quest. But instead he woke up at twilight, a horrible pain in his belly. He got to his knees, leaned over, and vomited.

He decided that it must have been the flesh, and made a mental note to avoid eating bushbuck in the future. He got up, began walking, felt queasy, ignored it and increased his pace, reaching twelve thousand feet before the nausea and the pain forced him to stop.

He tried to vomit again, but nothing came out. He lay down and tried to sleep, but his stomach began cramping, and he couldn't get comfortable. He tossed and turned, and finally fell into a restless slumber. He awoke before sunrise, tried once more to vomit, and began walking. He became increasingly dizzy, but he found a relatively straight branch on the ground, rid it of its leaves, and used it as a walking stick.

It took him the rest of the day to reach the tree line, and finally he walked out onto the glacier – and realized that far from being cold, he was uncomfortably warm. He walked another two hundred yards, and then collapsed.

What is the matter with me? he wondered. *I have never been sick a day of my life. I have conquered thirty worlds. What has happened?*

He thought about everything he had done since leaving the ship, and then it hit him: the standing water and the bushbuck's flesh. One or the other, possibly both, had native parasites that didn't bother the inhabitants of the mountain, but presented serious problems to which his system lacked any natural immunities. He didn't know if even his medical kit had a cure for them, but it didn't matter anyway, because the kit was back on Thandor IV.

And since he had no cure, all he could do was hope that eventually his body would find some way to combat the parasites, or that they would pass from his system, but either way he wasn't going to solve his problem by sitting here. He got painfully to his feet and began climbing, although he was becoming dizzier and sicker by the minute.

Finally he could go no farther. He did not even have the strength to lower himself gently to the ice. Instead he tossed his branch away and immediately collapsed, sprawled out awkwardly.

At least I won't freeze to death, he thought sardonically. *I'm burning up with fever.*

Another hour passed, and then another, and he realized that this spot was where he would die.

How ironic, he thought as his life ebbed away. *To conquer the greatest mountains and oceans, to kill the greatest beasts, and to finally succumb to something so small that I cannot even see it.*

He tried to smile as the thought crossed his mind, but it was too late even for that.

2038 A.D.

Bonnie Herrington walked over to me again, video camera in hand.

"Are you sure you don't want to be a little more positive about the man from Mars here?" she asked. "Everyone else is offering guesses about where he came from."

"Everyone else is a photographer, a sound man, a government official, a guide, and a bunch of porters," I said. "They're hardly trained to make definitive judgments about it."

"You don't really think he was born on Earth, do you?" she persisted.

"Is your camera off?"

"The camera's off, and my sound man's fifty feet away," she said, nodding her head toward Ray Glover.

"All right," I said. "No, this creature wasn't born on Earth. And of course he wasn't born on Mars. That leaves about ten billion other locations in this galaxy alone."

"And you won't take a guess as to where?"

"Only generically. It had to be a planet with a similar oxygen atmosphere and gravity. Not identical, but similar."

"Then why won't you say so for the camera?" persisted Bonnie.

I wanted to say *Because my word carries more weight than yours, and there's no sense lending any gravitas to these speculations until we know what we're dealing with.* But I knew it would offend, so I just shrugged and said, "Because these are speculations. Extraterrestrial conditions are not my field of expertise. We should wait until we can get some expert opinions."

She asked a few more questions, was clearly disappointed with the answers, and wandered back to where Glover was standing. Then Jim Donahue had us all stand together next to the body so he could take some group photos.

Finally Adrian Gorman suggested that there was nothing further to be done until I contacted my experts and they arrived.

I tapped the pocket that was holding my cell phone. "I'll be calling them in a few minutes."

"We could conceivably have them up here tomorrow," he said. "If they can charter a jet and be in Arusha by, say, noon, they can fly up to this spot via helicopter. There's enough level ground for a 'copter to set down without any problem."

Njobo nodded his agreement. "I will contact my superiors in Dodoma" – it was the first time he'd admitted that he *had* any superiors – "and they will determine when and where the body can be moved."

"It'll be dark in a couple of hours," noted Gorman. "There's no sense all of us freezing our asses off up here. We need one volunteer to guard the body, and I think we'll leave one of the porters up here too, in the unlikely event that you have to scare away a hyena or a jackal. The rest of us will go back to the huts where we left the tents and come back first thing in the morning."

Everyone was silent for a moment. I think they were all waiting for Gorman to volunteer. When it became obvious that he had no intention of staying on the glacier, I decided that Bonnie, Ray, Jim and even Gorman had already been working, so it made sense for me to offer to stay.

I raised a hand and said, without much enthusiasm, "I'll do it."

"Good," said Gorman, looking a bit relieved.

Muro spoke to the porters, and the big one I'd noticed before nodded his head, walked over, and spoke to Gorman in Swahili.

"Professor, this is Jaka. He'll be staying up here with you. We'll leave you some food and a bunch of thermal blankets you can wrap around yourselves. It won't feel like the Ritz, but you won't freeze to death."

"Sounds good enough," I said.

"Then we'll be on our way," said Gorman. "See you in the morning."

They marched off, and I pulled out my cell phone and began contacting my colleagues. Most were in America or Europe, but Ralph Galler was actually relatively nearby, in Nairobi. He told me that he'd drive to Arusha during the night, charter a helicopter at the small airport there, have it fly over the glacier, and home in on my cell phone's signal. He promised he'd be there at sunrise.

I tried to start a conversation with Jaka, but it was a very frustrating experience. His English simply wasn't up to the task. We each wrapped a thermal blanket around ourselves, grabbed some beef jerky from the supply kit, and ate in silence.

As the night closed in I tore some bushes out of the ground and tried to build a fire, but the wind kept blowing it out before it could really get started. I pulled the blanket more tightly around me, and tried not to pay attention to the freezing wind. To help keep awake I called some friends in England and America. Then, when I felt myself about to nod off, I broke the connection, and walked around the creature several times until the cold had thoroughly wakened me.

"How long until the helicopter gets here?" I asked Jaka as I was running out of tricks to keep alert.

"The sun should begin rising in another hour," he replied.

"Good," I said. "I thought morning would never come."

"It is on its way, alas," he said, starting to get to his feet.

I stared at him, frowning. "Your English is suddenly better," I said. "Where did a Chagga porter who lives on Kilimanjaro learn a word like 'alas'? And why would you use it?"

"Because I am tired of pretending, and very soon you will know the truth anyway."

"The truth?" I repeated. "What truth?"

"I'd hoped you'd be asleep by now," he said. "It would have been easier for both of us."

"Enough guessing games!" I snapped. "*What* would have been easier?"

"What I have to do."

"What the hell are you talking about?" I said, backing away from him.

"Just relax, Tony," he said. "If I may call you Tony? I'm not going to hurt you."

"Suddenly you don't sound like any porter or any Chagga I've ever met," I said accusingly.

He sighed deeply. "I really wish you'd fallen asleep."

I stared at him. "Are you here to steal our story?"

"No, Tony," he said. "I'm here to kill your story."

"Who *are* you?"

"Wrong question, Tony."

"What are you talking about?" I demanded.

"A better question would be: *what* am I?"

If I hadn't spent all day staring at the thing on the ground, I'd have had a lot more difficulty believing the thing in front of me.

"All right," I said. "*What* are you?"

"First let me tell you what I am not," he said. "I am not your enemy."

"Suppose you tell me your real name."

He smiled sadly as the first rays of sunlight appeared on the horizon. "You couldn't pronounce it."

"Do you really look like this?" I asked.

"Only when I choose to," he replied.

"A shape-changer?" I said. "I don't believe it."

"I only have one shape," he answered. "What you see is an image I project."

Suddenly the full impact of my situation hit me, and I backed away a few steps. "Now that I know what you are, are you going to kill me?" I asked.

"Of course not, Tony."
"So you've just come for your friend," I said.
"He was not my friend."

WHAT NOBODY SAW

"Then why are you here?" I asked. "Was he a criminal?"

An amused smile. "No, Tony. He was a pet."

"A *what?*"

"You know how your miners used to carry a small bird – a canary, I believe it was called – into a mine? It wasn't as strong as the miners. If there were any poisonous fumes, it would collapse first, and that was a signal to them to get out of the mine." He paused. "This was the same principle. We are a starfaring race, but although we breathe an oxygen/nitrogen atmosphere very similar to your own, not all planets are hospitable to us. There are certain inert elements, certain ultra-violet rays, certain microbes, that our systems cannot handle. This is not unusual. When your race reaches the stars, you will encounter the same thing. We can analyze samples all we want, but the surest way remains using our version of a canary." He smiled sadly. "This one made it only four months. I have to take him home so we can find out exactly what killed him and whether we can come up with a means of counteracting it."

"Why was he – and your race – here at all?" I asked.

"Why do you have children?" he replied. "We have a desire to spread our seed throughout the galaxy, but only on worlds where we will be welcomed, where we can live in peace with the inhabitants. Earth might have been such a world, had my pet lived."

"How long has he been here?" I asked.

"Not quite a century," replied Jaka.

"And you're just coming for him now?" I said, frowning.

"None of us is permitted to stay here more than three months," he said. "In fact, only I have been here more than once, because it truly was my pet. One of us has been on every expedition on this side of the mountain since the day he died. But there were very few expeditions back then, and far more snow than there is today. We knew he was here, and we knew he was hidden beneath the snow and ice, so we were not worried that some lone man would find him. It would take an expedition, because almost no one goes up on the glacier alone, and since no one was looking for him and no one would be digging through the ice for him, we knew that he almost certainly wouldn't show up until the periodic warming trend began melting the ice cap."

"And what happens now?" I asked.

"Now," he said, "I take him home. We need to know why he died. There is an outside possibility that it was not something inimical to us. We hope that we may still be able to reach a friendly accommodation with you at some point in the future, when you are a little better prepared for visitors."

He withdrew a small device from a pocket and began manipulating it.

"I am summoning my ship," he explained. "It was much farther up the mountain. I would have moved it had our party gone that high." He stood still for a moment, staring at the device. "It is here now," he said. He manipulated it again, and his ship suddenly appeared about a hundred yards away.

"It's like magic!" I said.

"The cloaking mechanism bends the light around it, so it becomes invisible to the eye. But any instrument designed to detect metal would have found it." He put the device away. "I am truly sorry that you were awake for this. I possess nothing that can wipe the experience from your memory, nor would I use it if I had such a thing. But I strongly advise you not to mention it. No one will believe you, and you will lose all credibility within your field."

There was no sense arguing with him. He was right.

"What about your tracks?" I said. "It will be obvious that you picked up the body and carried it to your ship."

"There are hundreds of tracks here. Every one of you stood next to it at one time or another. Mine will just be added to the rest. Besides," he added with a smile, "what ship? No one else has seen it, and I will be gone in a handful of minutes."

"But we have films!" I said.

He withdrew another tiny mechanism from a different pocket. "Not any longer," he said, holding it up. "Bonnie Herrington and Jim Donahue will find that they stood next to a very powerful magnetic field. They won't know when or where, but they will know that it wiped their film and pictures."

"But why?" I asked. "You're getting the body. Why not leave us with proof that it existed?"

"If I did, and those films and photos gained credibility, your race would drop everything else and concentrate on reaching the stars. You'll get there one day, but you have more immediate problems facing you."

"Isn't that for us to decide?" I said.

"Not any longer."

"Some of us know," I said. "We'll tell others."

"They won't believe you," replied Jaka. "But I will soften the blow for you."

"What are you talking about?" I demanded.

"You shall see in a minute."

He lifted the creature's body – the *real* Jaka was obviously much stronger than the image he projected – and loaded it into his ship. I made no attempt to stop him. How could I? It was *his* pet, and he was far stronger than me.

A moment later he emerged with a dead, mummified leopard in his arms. He carried it over to the spot where the creature had been and laid it down on the snow.

"What's this all about?" I asked.

"Congratulations," he said with a smile. "Your party has accomplished its purpose and found Hemingway's leopard."

"They found an alien," I said stubbornly.

"One story will make you famous, one will receive nothing but ridicule," he said. "What you tell them is your decision."

His ship took off a few minutes later.

I looked down the mountain and saw my party approaching. They had left behind an alien creature, and were about to find a leopard in its place. I could tell them how it came to be there, but I doubted they'd believe me until they realized that every other possible explanation was even more unbelievable. Njobo probably hadn't contacted his superiors yet; he enjoyed being the sole authority figure too much. And Bonnie, Ray and Jim had been paid to take photos of Hemingway's leopard, so while this would cost them a better story, it wouldn't cost them any money. The only person who had mentioned our discovery to any outsiders was me, and I could contact the handful of people I'd called and say that someone had pulled a joke on me, or I'd been drunk, or anything else that might get them mad but wouldn't make them doubt my explanation. It all depended on the complicity of my party. Just how much were they going to insist upon telling the truth?

I could hear Ralph Galler's chopper approaching the mountain, and I deactivated my cell phone to buy us a few more minutes to reach a decision before he landed.

As the others reached me, eager to once again see the most remarkable discovery of their lives, I wondered which story we would tell when the helicopter arrived.

www.ingramcontent.com/pod-product-compliance
Lightning Source LLC
Chambersburg PA
CBHW020620130626
46552CB00003B/1059